I0891601

THE RAIN SAID 'SAMSARA'

Mary Reynard Liss

Mary Reynard Liss

THE RAIN SAID 'SAMSARA'

MARY REYNARD LISS

This is a work of fiction.

ISBN paperback: 978-1-958156-14-8
ISBN ebook: 978-1-958156-15-5
ISBN audiobook: 978-1-958156-16-2
Registered WGA 2024
Published by Lexographic Press, Hyde Park, Chicago
lexographicpress.com

I dedicate this book to my beautiful, remarkable, hardworking mother, Betty Jane Petelle; To my brilliant and charismatic husband, Ted Liss; and to my Rockstar brother, Robert Klopp.

All of them gone too soon, but forever alive in my heart, and in the hearts of the many who loved them.

My deepest gratitude to Joseph Gandurski for his enlightening consultations, his patient mentorship, his technical skills, and his enthusiastic encouragement.

Heartfelt thanks to Edith Klopp, whose generous editorial assistance made it possible for this novel to progress to its final draft.

Special thanks to Kathryn Becker, Rebecca Brandt, Amy Green, Dalene Meyers, and Karen Minnis, for their invaluable feedback and support.

Mary Reynard Liss

PART ONE

SILENT SONGS

1

1970's: The roads between Wisconsin and Chicago

After a day of antiquing in the boondocks of Wisconsin, Marissa left the highway and chose an unfamiliar route home. She thought the small paved road would provide a picturesque ride through the countryside, a welcome departure from the humdrum highway. After a while the paved road turned into a small dirt road, which wound endlessly through what became a barren stretch of land. The deserted landscape showed no signs of inhabitation, and offered not one familiar sight. In the distance she saw veins of lightening discharging through the twilight sky, followed by the sound of rolling thunder. She was getting nervous. It was getting dark and a storm was brewing. Unexpectedly a brilliant flash of lightening lit up the entire sky. Its primordial splendor stunned her, stripping her of all defenses, uniting her to the shockwave that caused the explosive crack of thunder, which followed seconds later. The classical music that she had been listening to on the radio was now lost. It had been replaced by the chaotic sounds of many channels bleeding through static. A haunting, operatic soprano voice could be heard, then the inspired intonations of a theological discussion, then the dissonant chords, pounding drums and primitive shouting of a rock and roll band. They all blended together, none of them able to sustain their individual current. Other sounds and voices cried out, but they were lost in indistinguishable noise.

Suddenly, there in the middle of nowhere, on the side of the abandoned dirt road, stood a forgotten glass phone booth. It was a strange and melancholy sight. She turned off the radio and stopped the car. She stared at it, fascinated, and then felt compelled to enter it. She stepped out of her car into the breezy, ozone filled evening air. To her surprise the booth's door folded open easily, welcoming her inside. She stood in the glass enclosure looking out onto the strobing landscape. High on ozone and adrenaline, she felt transported to a place where there was no measurement of time. The mingling voices from the radio still resonated in her body, filling her with a longing for something she couldn't identify: something familiar, but just out of reach. Her senses turned inward to an awareness of currents resonating deep inside her, imprinted upon her soul, lit up, and searching for expression.

Rousing herself from this mesmerized state, she fumbled through her purse searching for loose change. She dropped the coins into the slot of the pay phone, dialed the rotary dial and waited for him to answer. As the phone rang, lightning struck, momentarily blinding her, accompanied by menacing thunder. She almost hung up, thinking that she had better be on her way before the rain hit and turned the road to mud. And then he answered.

"Yeah," was all he said. The sound of his voice intoxicated her.

"Hey tough guy," she said into the receiver. "It's thundering and lightning and I'm thinking about being in your arms!"

They both laughed. They spoke for only a few minutes. She told him of her day antiquing in the boondocks of Wisconsin. She described to him her adventure that had gone awry: the road that had led her so far off the highway and the solitary phone booth that she had come upon.

"I'm in this phone booth in the middle of nowhere in the middle of a spectacular light show," she began. "And I'm the only one here to witness it! So I had to call and share to it with you."

Another bolt of lightning struck close by.

"The phone booth just lit up," she told him. "Just like I light up every time you touch me."

"I'd like to be in that booth with you right now Baby," he began.

"I'd love to hear more, you sexy man, but there's a storm coming so I better get going."

He could hear the thunder.

"Hurry up and get to the highway," he said, his tone changing to one of concern. "Go back the way you came. Get to safety. Don't drive to the North Side. Come to my place. It's closer"

Quarter sized raindrops started to splatter on the glass walls of the booth as she stepped back out onto the dirt road. The large raindrops were already imprinting their wet image in the dust. She adjusted the headlights of her car to 'bright', turned the car around, and drove off into the darkness, with her windshield wipers on high. The thunder was right overhead now bringing with it a sudden cloudburst. The rain came down in a deluge. She was scared and so called upon the protection of the angels to see her home safely. She fixated on the narrow road, which was quickly turning to mud. The windshield wipers rapidly switched back and forth from a blinding veil of rain to brief moments of clarity. She clung to the clarity. She wanted to speed but knew she had better not. Instead, her mind raced. Her level of receptivity was heightened. The cloudburst seemed to be bathing her in feeling tones. Fleeting memories flooded her senses. The din of the falling rain took on a frequency of its own. Out of its ambient sound a word was formed.

The rain said "SAMSARA".

Marissa knew this word. It meant reincarnation and the resolution of karma. She strained every sensory resource in her being hoping to hear another word. But no other word was spoken. Now it was the thunder that dominated the soundscape. Its intensity made the road beneath her car tremble, conjuring up an image of the thundering of horse's hoofs on an old forgotten dirt road.

2

Black Forest of Germany: 1600's

The Aristocrat's carriage raced through the dark forest, driven by his trusted friend, a devout young cleric. A patchwork of moonlight shone down through the canopy of trees, revealing quick glimpses of the galloping horses, the jostled coach and the driver's determined face. His green eyes blazed as his thick, golden-brown hair was blown back by the thundering speed of the horses. Inside the coach a young gentleman protectively cradled an infant. This journey was a matter of life and death.

An arrangement had been made. The young gentleman had sent no servant, but brought the newborn girl to the isolated cloister of the Carmelite nuns himself. The Holy Mother was waiting as he stepped from the carriage to stand in the dimly-lit courtyard. He could feel the silent prayers of centuries all around him. They passed through him knowing that at this moment, he was not solid, but made of dust. He held the infant to his heart and wept. He then gently put the child into the arms of the Holy Mother, wordlessly, for the Carmelites were a hermetic order, which observed a vow of silence. He quickly turned and disappeared back into the carriage and then into winter's night. He must return home before anyone thought him gone for too long. The pounding of the horse's hoofs turned into a soft echo in the cold air as his coach sped away.

Although an infant, the child had felt the thundering of the horse's hoofs in her small body, the warmth of the man's embrace, and his wet tears, now cold upon her face in the night air. A pre-language knowledge of his love and sorrow were forever imprinted upon her soul. Their separation might have been traumatic if not for the sacred atmosphere of the convent and the voices of the otherwise-silent Carmelites raised in the vesper song. In the Holy Mother's arms, the child felt a current pass through her tiny body. This powerful force found a home in the innocence of her new soul, and filled her with a resonance that connected her to all of creation. This became the blueprint of her life.

As the young gentleman's coach rode into the night, he gradually felt the energy of the cloister subsiding. The sacred atmosphere was palpable, even for miles outside of their gates. With distance, his anguish slowly turned into a profound sense of relief.

His name was Robert. He had just saved his sister's life. Their cruel father, The Duke of Mecklenburg, would forever believe that she had died at birth along with her poor mother, the unlucky impoverished peasant girl who had been the victim of the Duke's secret obsessions. To save himself from scandal the Duke had ordered the infant killed at birth, but Robert, overhearing his father's murderous utterances, had quickly devised this plan to save her.

Now, Robert took a deep, sustaining breath. All was well. His sister was safe in the care of the Carmelites. He closed his eyes and whispered a prayer of gratitude as the carriage thundered through the Black Forest, back to Mecklenburg.

The driver was his dearest boyhood friend, now an apostolic cleric named Father Michael. It was he who had made the arrangements with the Carmelites and would continue to act as Robert's messenger, delivering alms regularly for Gretchen's care and for the support of the convent.

As Robert sat in the carriage praying, he knew he might never see his sister again. He had asked only one thing from the Holy Mother: that the child be named Gretchen, after her own poor mother. He spoke her name softly, once, knowing that, for her safety, he must never speak it again. He would never forget her.

Gretchen was a blessing to the nuns and they to her. In their world all were loved equally and unquestionably, and so she never knew fear or loneliness. It was not predetermined that she would join their order. When she came of age, she could rely upon the illumination of her own heart to make that decision. No demands were made of her outside of those made in the upbringing of a child. Because the nuns did not speak Gretchen did not speak, although it was not forbidden to her. The only human sounds she heard were those of the nun's voices raised in the vesper song. From infancy she was steeped in these sounds. And as the first few years of her life passed, their music became a bridge between heaven and earth to her. Their voices intoning the pitches of the hymns delivered her into the mind of the Creator where all was perfect, complete and joyful. And so as she grew, she sang. At first she made only humming sounds but eventually forming the words to the hymns. This was how she learned language. She was taught to read, and write and the other necessities, by writing on a slate which she carried with her always.

Those whom she lived among were discalced Carmelites, meaning barefoot. They had taken vows of poverty, chastity, obedience and silence. Their lives were devoted to continuous communion with God. Their mantra was "Enter into the Infinite Space". They were as self-sufficient as possible but also relied on alms from distant, devout Christian communities and aristocrats to provide for their upkeep. Their convent was deep in the German wilderness away from the secular communities. The nearest city was Mecklenburg. Occasionally a person on horseback, or an aristocrat in a carriage would appear with contributions for them, along with written requests for their continuing prayers and blessings. These alms were given in silence, pushed through a curtain that sequestered the Carmelite nun on the other side, who then added them to the community chest. Other than that, entrance into the cloister was forbidden.

When Gretchen was four, she began to work in the garden and help in the kitchen. She sang as she worked. Her connection to the Lord through her pure voice delighted her co-workers and they never found her to be a distraction from their meditations. At seven she could scrub floors and do laundry. Whatever chores were assigned to her she did with joy, singing and humming as she performed them.

She loved her small stone room where, after kneeling at the foot of her wooden bed in silent prayer, she was put to sleep each night. Prayer was as natural to her as breathing. She lived in a world where communion with the Creator was present in every second, not relegated to moments of love or separate acts of devotion. She would not have understood that.

As she grew up, time was made for her to wander through the forests that surrounded the convent. There she learned about the animals. Their communication, with humans and with one another, was telepathic. The Carmelites were vegetarians so she had no knowledge that others ate animals and could not even conceive of such a thing. The animals had no fear of her. She was connected to them and they to her through their hearts. She would play with them in the warm summer and spring, and tend to them in the cold winter when they needed her help.

Gretchen knew how to listen to the evolving elemental energies of nature. The smooth stones that lie under the water of the creek spoke to her with the whispers of ancient voices, which lived inside them. The water in the creek babbled of the transformative powers of kindness, while showing Gretchen her reflection, gently shimmering in its ripples. The trees sang songs of perpetual guardianship, and their breath replenished the earth. The drowsy flowers liked to chatter and hum when she awakened them and they showered her with healing, loving energy. When the wind blew, she heard music. A symphony, where a chaos of natural sounds synthesized into a divine order that filled not only her ears, but her heart and soul. This cacophony filled her prayers. Her meditations overflowed with gratitude to the creator for this divine creation. Her life was blessed. She wanted for nothing. She was a conduit for everything.

3

Michael was a serious child with a devotional nature. His family of eight was poor, and his mother often sick. His father was hard working, but exhausted and broken by the exploitation of his labor at the hands of the wealthy landowner, the Duke of Mecklenburg. It was the 1600's, a time when the Duke controlled every aspect of the peasants' lives. Mecklenburg was surrounded by primeval forests and cut off from the rest of Germany. This isolation and independence from their neighbors assured that there was no judgment of the Duke and his treacherous ways.

When Michael was eleven years old, he met Robert and they became close friends. Robert was the kindhearted son of the Duke. His father had no compassion for the families in need and exploited them at every opportunity. When he was told of his son's friendship with Michael he forbade Robert to ever see him again. But Robert had the strength to defy his father. He was a clever and sensitive boy whose devout Catholic mother, Elizabeth, had taught him right from wrong. She was a lovely woman with luminous brown eyes and gentle ways. Robert looked a lot like her having inherited her brown eyes and dignified features. He also emulated her behavior, learning from her his obligation as a nobleman to give alms to the church and to help the poor. This, his mother insisted upon, over the objections of the Duke, the man she had been forced to marry to consolidate property. And yet her husband would enjoy the credit given him for these donations, when his name was announced from the pulpit of the great Cathedral where they attended Sunday services.

Michael and Robert were true friends. Their connection had been forged through the goodness of their open hearts, fun loving spirits and observant wits. They were kindred spirits from their first meeting. Michael, having a beautiful voice, had been selected by the choirmaster of the great cathedral to sing in the choir. He was seated alongside Robert, who had greeted him warmly. He didn't care that Michael was barefoot and wore shabby clothes. The two became inseparable. When Michael stopped coming to Sunday Mass, Robert became worried. He traveled to Michael's village where he found him sick, and his whole family starving. And so Robert brought them food. He brought Michael's family whatever food he could manage to take from his household without being detected. He did it himself for he knew that if he were to be found out, anyone who had helped him would be severely beaten.

Michael's family shared whatever Robert brought them with their neighbors. But even with Robert's help they would have starved to death if not for a traveling apostolic cleric named Father Theodore. He had come to their village on horseback with a wooden cart from which he fed the hungry families. Much of the food came from the garden of the Carmelite convent that was deep in the forest. Father Theodore went to each rambled-down shack with their dirt floors, ministering to the sick.

Witnessing this man of faith and compassion was to Michael like witnessing a manifestation of God's grace alive and animated through a human being. He told Robert of this holy man and together, of one mind, they made a plan. Robert would tell his mother, Elizabeth, of Father

Theodore and appeal to her to meet him. Upon meeting him and seeing his godliness, she would respond to his fervent request to grant him alms in perpetuity to expand his ministry. Their righteous plan came to fruition and with the help of Elizabeth this became a reality.

Seeing the families around him being fed and cared for when sick stirred Michael's soul to a "Quickening" that brought him to his knees. Deep in prayer he felt the power of the Holy Spirit descend upon him. From that moment on he worked tirelessly alongside the holy man and pledged his life to following in his footsteps. Despair, poverty, suffering and exploitation had been emblazoned upon his innocent soul. And now, at the age of eleven, through the anointment of the Holy Spirit, he became an intercessor, helping to bring relief and restoration to those bodies and souls in need. This became the blueprint of his life. He traveled with Father Theodore, was taught by him, and eventually took the vows of poverty, obedience and chastity himself. When the cleric became old and infirm, Michael carried on his ministry.

And now, seven years later, Robert entrusted him with the secret care of his beloved sister.

Once a month Michael would ride his horse through the forest to deliver alms from Robert to the nuns. He never saw Gretchen, but he often heard the singing of a child, and he knew it was her. Being a singer himself, he was well versed in the music of the church. He often waited outside the convent's gates to listen to the nuns singing vespers. Gradually he heard a new voice emerge, often singing solos, and he knew it was Gretchen. The music that stirred his spirit the most was the *Salve Regina*. As he sat horseback, outside of the gates, he would reverently listen. And then, thinking that the nuns could not hear him, he would join in:

"Angels, all your praises bring,
Earth and heaven with us sing,
All creation echoing,
Salve, salve, salve Regina."

But the nuns could hear his beautiful, rich voice. Gretchen heard him, and she knew that his beautiful voice, blending with theirs, was a visitation from the Holy Spirit.

Although forbidden to speak her name, over the years Michael, in secret encounters, had told her brother of the girl's angelic voice. It was in the fifteenth year of their separation that Robert did something he had never done before. He gave Michael a gift for her. It was a collection of very old sacred music used in the liturgy of the Mass. In past generations it had been a family treasure, but had long since been forgotten about. Worn from the loving use from another time, Robert now found it, thick with dust, on a high shelf that had not been disturbed in decades. Their library was extensive and this old book would not be missed. Robert knew it belonged in the hands of his sister, to be sung by her in praise and shared with the Carmelites. And so he lovingly wrapped it in a piece of rich fabric. A tapestry made of the finest silken threads of silver, gold and purple. He entrusted it to Michael who devotedly obliged to deliver it.

4

It was unusually hot for a day in early Spring. It had been cold and raining hard for several days. Now the sun was bright and it's heat excessive. The road that wound through the wilderness was muddy and difficult for Michael's horse to navigate, so he decided to ride through the forest. The forest floor was wet and fragrant, as was the bark of the trees. Hazy shafts of light shone down through their canopy, which provided relief from the heat of the sun. He slowed his horse's pace down to a walk. He had traveled through the forest before, but today everything looked different. It was as if he had ridden into a heavenly region, lit by the Lord. The alms for the Carmelites were secure in his saddlebag, as was the protectively wrapped book of music for Gretchen. The harsh weather had not damaged it. As Michael went deeper into the forest he came upon the creek. He saw that the animals had left their hiding places to bask on the warm rocks beside it. His horse moved slowly so as not to scare them away. Michael smiled, knowing that the chill of the cold rainy days was leaving their small bodies as they lay contentedly on the warm rocks. The chill left his body as well. The day before the creek had been turbulent, with the deluge of the rain causing rushing torrents. But now as he traveled alongside it, it was still and peaceful. The air was moist as the water evaporated from the damp forest floor. As he breathed it in, it seemed to envelop a faint soft voice. As his horse plodded along, leaving its hoofs imprinted in the debris alongside the creek, Father Michael realized that the soft voice had been that of someone singing in the distance. As it grew louder, he stilled his horse and listened. He knew it was Gretchen. Nothing stirred. Everything was so still and silent that it seemed the whole forest was in a thrall wanting only to listen to her song. The animals were still, letting her music pass over them.

Not too far away Gretchen stood barefoot in the creek singing a holy song. The smooth stones beneath her feet told her of Father Michael's arrival. The horse's hoofs had sent vibrations through the water that stirred the stones and made them whisper. Although she had never seen him and didn't know his name, she knew who it was. The Holy Spirit had left his signature upon her heart. She looked at her wavering reflection in the brook and for the first time wondered what it was like for another to see her.

Not wanting to disrespect the rules of the convent by approaching her, Michael knew he must find his way back to the road. The mud had dried significantly in the sun, so he rode the rest of the way on his usual route. Although a chaste and devout holy man, the perfect happiness of listening to Gretchen singing in the forest did not escape him. As he rode to the convent he meditated on her song.

The road was a longer way around than the way through the woods. It was mid-afternoon before he arrived at the convent. The nuns had completed the morning's work and were performing their solitary prayers and meditations. In the bright glare of the sun the nun coming to open the gates seemed to be floating towards him. As he dismounted and walked to the door she kindly tended to his thirsty horse. All was still and quiet until the bell above the door he passed through rang, summoning a nun to the area behind the curtain. He pushed through the bundle of alms first. He could hear the usual sounds of the bundle being lifted and moved. He then pushed through the package for Gretchen with a simple written message: "This is a book of music for Gretchen". There was a long pause. A slate was pushed through the curtain with the message: "Please wait".

He obediently sat on a wooden chair by a small table and prayed. After a short time, to his surprise, the Holy Mother entered. He had not seen her for fifteen years and she was now almost eighty years old. In her delicate hands she carried the book. She moved with great efficiency and grace as she joined him at the table. She set the book down before him. Even under a vow of silence a Carmelite may speak if absolutely necessary. The Holy Mother had made a decision. Without wasting a word she spoke to Michael. Her voice was low and gentle.

"Gretchen is of an age where she will be ready to decide if she wishes to join our order. I would like her to have the opportunity to speak with someone about the secular world. You are the one who has the information she might be seeking. Take this book of music to her. Tell her whatever she wishes to know. But do not burden her with what she does not wish to know."

With an elegant motion of her hand she gestured to a large carved wooden door. "She is in the chapel." The Holy Mother rose and swiftly disappeared behind the curtain. It was the first time she had spoken since taking her vows.

Michael often had encounters with people of all ages and states of mind. He often spent hours speaking with them, counseling them, soothing them, or just listening to them. So this was not an unusual task for him. He picked up the wrapped book and quietly pushed open the heavy door. On the other side was an exquisite, small chapel with a single stained glass window. It was round, and at its center was the image of the Blessed Mother Mary, surrounded by rays of light that formed a Mandala. The bright light shining through the window flooded the chapel with muted shades of gold, blue, rose and green. Gretchen was praying before a carved statue of St. Theresa at the side of the altar. The votive candles from the shrine illuminated her face. He saw that her features were finely chiseled, her hair long and dark, her skin pale, and her eyes luminous and gray. As she stood and walked towards him, he walked forward to the altar to greet her. He saw that although she was not tall, she had stature. Like the other nuns, she was very thin. When she turned her gaze to him, it was enigmatic. Direct yet far away. She saw that he was tall and strong with thick golden brown hair and gentle green eyes. As he began to speak Gretchen could see herself reflected in his eyes in a way unfamiliar, yet deeply moving.

"Gretchen, I am Father Michael," he began. He indicated the book in his hands and said, "I have been sent here to give you a gift. "

There was something in his voice and gaze that fully engaged Gretchen. Not accustomed to the spoken word, Gretchen listened in the only way she knew how. To her his words were a cascading soundscape of images and feeling tones. His voice rose up from the ground, as if the earth was speaking. Words were different when spoken. Her thoughts raced to keep pace with her expanding understanding of Father Michael's purpose. She comprehended that his words were codifying impulses and events and placing them into her mind. Missing the clarity of musical tones, his words were an attempt to inspire in thought the energy fields that musical tones contained and informed of wordlessly. She could feel that he was a man who used words to heal and teach. His words were born of pure intention and therefore a prayer. She began to understand who he was and his place in the outside world. It was a world she knew nothing of. He used words to inspire understanding and to teach people to find their place in life, as he was doing now as he spoke to her. As he spoke, she understood how his words captured thoughts, and how the people he spoke to gained identity through an exchange of these words. When used by him, words dispelled fear and created community.

Through his words she felt her brother's love and understood what he had done for her. She realized that eventually, when her safety was assured, she could have a life in the outside world, if she chose that life. When Father Michael fell silent, she extended her hands to accept the gift of the book of music. As she unwrapped it, she felt the threads of the tapestry beneath her fingers. Each thread sang of love and imparted to her the memory of her brother. She held the book to her heart and was transported back to the courtyard on that cold winter's evening. She felt the warmth of her brother's embrace and his tears upon her face; his tears, and now hers. Crying was out of the ordinary for Gretchen. But these tears were not an expression of sorrow but of joy. She looked up at Father Michael. She was filled with gratitude.

"Is there anything more you would like to know?' he asked. "Is there anything you would like to tell me?"

A voice welled up in Gretchen and found its expression not in words, but in the familiarity of song. In an outpouring of love she sang to him the *Salve Regina.*

> *"Hail Holy Queen enthroned above,*
> *Oh Maria!*
> *Hail Queen of Mercy and of Love,*
> *Oh Maria!*
> *He understood that this was her gift to him, and he sang with her.*
> *Triumph, all ye Cherubim,*
> *Sing with us, ye Seraphim,*
> *Heaven and earth resound the hymn.*
> *Salve, salve, salve Regina!"*

Their combined voices filled the chapel and rang throughout the convent with such purity that they became part of the prayers of the nuns. When the final note had been sung and its echo had faded from the chapel, Father Michael took Gretchen's hand and held it warmly for only a second. He then turned and left.

Gretchen stood alone before the altar. His rough large hand had enfolded hers. His touch had stunned her. An energy she had never known flooded her body. It rose from the earth and passed through her with such power that it drove her to her knees. Attempting to ground it in prayer she clasped her hands together. She felt in her hands the thousands of hands that had reached out to Father Michael and that he had clasped as their rescuer. It was his hand that reached out to them when all hope was gone. She felt the misery and pain that Father Michael had absorbed and dispelled, and some which he would forever carry with him. Unable to contain this force she was driven downward to a prostrate position upon the chapel floor. In his touch was a strength that most are never called upon to demonstrate, but upon which most lives depend.

She felt his spirit now, towering over her like an archangel. She felt her body changing...her cells becoming liquid and transforming into exquisite crystalline shapes. She was being tuned to his spirit. She had been cloistered away in safety and prayer her whole life. She had lived in the sublime mind of the Creator. Her life had been a heaven on earth. She was now being tuned to a spirit who had not been sheltered. One who knew suffering, anguish, and treachery. A spirit, who in response to these inequities offered protection, healing and compassion. Father Michael brought the earth to heaven. She understood. Their spirits melded in perfect harmony: she bringing heaven to earth, and he bringing earth to heaven. The dynamic of their union brought her to the "Infinite Space." In that space her song expanded into one so pure, focused and subtle that it became silent. It became continuous and perfect communion with God, grounded now in her soul's purpose. It was a purpose that illuminated her heart. She lay on the floor in a rapture for a long time. When she arose she was forever changed.

There was great joy at the convent when Gretchen took her vows.

Their child of God now came to the Holy Mother and her community with a mature soul and an illuminated heart. She took the vows of poverty, obedience, chastity and perpetual silence, of the Hermetic Discalced Carmelite Order. She took the name Sister Mary Therese. Her continuous prayers were sent out to help the entire world, but they were fueled and focused by her connection to Father Michael's soul and his work in the outside world. When she dug in the garden, she felt Father Michael's touch in the rich soil. When water slid between her fingers, she felt the rush of his energy passing through her. She felt his essence in the air she breathed, in the heat of the sunlight and the shimmering of the rain. When the snowflakes fell, she meditated upon the crystalline beauty of her transformation, brought on by his warm hand around hers. In the blooming of the flowers she recognized the breaking open of her heart and soul. She knew him in the Infinite Space. He was there with her always. He had brought her there with one touch. Gretchen never spoke again. Her song had become so expansive that it could only be expressed in total silence. She no longer sang. This was not a cause of sadness for her community for they knew that she had become one with the Eternal Song. Her life was blessed. She had never experienced evil, but through the knowledge imparted to her through Father Michael she had been chosen by God to send the silent songs of her prayers out to combat it, and to intercede for those it afflicted.

Father Michael continued to bring alms to the convent and to sing at their gates. But he never saw Gretchen again. He knew she had joined their order and was now Sister Mary Therese. But he thought of her as Gretchen. He listened to the nuns sing the holy songs from the book he had delivered. But he never heard Gretchen sing again. He could feel the ascension of her soul into perpetual silence. Father Michael and all of the nuns could feel Gretchen's silent song embracing their individual voices joining them together into one voice.

For the rest of his ministry Father Michael felt the power of

Gretchen's prayers with him always. They fortified him and gave him strength. Every cell in his body remembered the union of their voices on that day in the chapel. When he prayed, that memory brought him to the union of their souls in the service of God. He knew God had blessed him with Gretchen, his soul's companion. As he grew older his receptivity to her essence became more keenly experienced. He felt her pure love surrounding him always. He felt the richness of her spirit protecting him, as the rich tapestry fabric had protected the book of holy music he had delivered to her. Her spirit warmed him when he was cold and healed him when he was sick. When he grew too old to travel, he sat in the sun and quietly sang the *Salve Regina* feeling her near in the deep contentment of his soul.

When it was Gretchen's time to leave the earth she was surrounded by her beloved community. She lay down on the same wooden bed she had slept in since a child. Now, it was her deathbed. She was not sick. It was her sixty seventh year and her spirit no longer clung to her flesh. The earth was no longer her home. All was quiet, as if the forest and animals were reverent, knowing that she was departing. The nuns gazed upon her lovingly, for to be countenanced by her was to be illuminated. Now in her final moments she blazed with light, as the thin membrane that had confined her spirit to her body melted away. Her open eyes glowed as she took her last breath. As she exhaled, she uttered one prayerful word. The only word she had ever spoken.

She whispered: "Michael."

An ecstatic charge of energy filled the room and Gretchen was gone before the name she had uttered. It lingered in the air, embraced by a slight echo, and was then absorbed into the stone walls, which would forever whisper his name.

In the early morning, not long after Gretchen's death, Father Michael woke from a beautiful dream. A second later he couldn't remember what it had been about, but it left him filled with happiness.

The persistent rain of the last few days had lulled him into inactivity, but now the sun was shining, and he felt good. He wanted to go for a walk in the woods nearby the modest stone house that he now occupied with several other clerics. He was very old. He walked slowly. His body had become frail and pain ridden from a lifetime of riding his horse on rough roads through bad weather, often pulling a rickety old cart laden with supplies, to minister to his beloved brothers and sisters.

As he reached the forest creek, he lowered himself onto a long flat rock lit by a shaft of sun. The heat of the rock soothed his sore muscles and he breathed a sigh of relief and gratitude. The forest animals were all around him. The water of the creek seemed to greet him fondly with the moisture of a soft kiss upon his brow. He smiled. The sun was bright, so he closed his eyes. He laid there in perfect peace for a long while. Then within his deep meditation he felt a small soft hand enfold his. He thought he opened his eyes, but he did not. Even so, he saw Gretchen sitting on the rock beside him. She was as he first saw her in the chapel: young, pale, with long dark hair glistening in the bright sun, her gray eyes looking into his with infinite kindness. He took a deep breath, joyful at the sight of her. As he exhaled, he dissolved into the brilliance of the sun with his hand in hers. A gentle breeze stirred the creek and the trees tenderly, as the small animals, who had borne witness to Michael's passing, climbed up onto the rock where he rested, and laid close to him, to feel the warmth of his body, as it left him.

PART TWO

THE FLIGHT OF THE WHITE BIRD

1

1970's: the Highway between Wisconsin and Chicago

Marissa had carefully traversed the muddy road and found her way back to the highway. Even with the windshield wipers on high it was still hard to see in the torrential downpour. As other cars passed her they created waves of water that rose off the pavement drenching her car and making it seem, momentarily, as if she was underwater. The bright headlights from the approaching cars were aimed right at her eyes and came at her like magnesium flashes. The wind had become so powerful that it was blowing her car sideways. And yet she piloted the vehicle deftly, driving down a highway that only hours before had been mundane, before the confluence of elemental energies and technology had made it spectacular with atmosphere, and fraught with the danger of machines. She was driving past an area of small towns that had been there since the turn of the century. The residents were in their modest homes, waiting out the storm. She felt their peace and was again filled with a longing for a vaguely remembered home. She intuitively turned the radio back on half hoping that she would hear another word, this time spoken in the static. To her surprise the static was gone and her classical station's signal was clear again. It was broadcasting her favorite opera: *La Traviata*. She drew a deep breath. It calmed her. It seemed the perfect soundtrack to give shape and meaning to the intangibles that she was being bombarded with.

2
USA, Europe, Middle East- Late 1800's thru Mid-1900s

"It's just like heaven," six-year-old Robert told her excitedly. "If you want ice cream you just walk up and say 'I want some ice cream', and *they give it to you*! If you want a hot dog you just walk up and say, 'I want a hot dog!' Anything you want you can have: pie, cake, candy, anything!"

His excitement was contagious. His four–year-old sister Theresa couldn't wait for this amazing event called the Decoration Day Picnic. It was to take place at Timber Lake, a heavily wooded, secluded area with a picnic ground and a lake that you could swim in!

Their father, Claude Berto, was sponsoring this celebration for his employees and the whole town was invited. He was the heir to his grandfather's fortune, amassed by the making of carved wooden clocks, and the importing of furniture from the Black Forest of Germany. Theresa and Robert didn't see much of their father. He was often away in Europe on business trips. Although Theresa could not have put this into words, she was relieved when he wasn't at home. Robert felt the same way.

Their mother, Greta, was a very beautiful and fun-loving woman who was called "flighty" by all who knew her. She could not concentrate or hold a thought in her head for more than a few seconds. But the townspeople loved her charm, her sparkling blue eyes, and her stunning Slavic beauty.

All the boys in their small Wisconsin town had been smitten with her. But when, eight years ago, their father turned his attention to her, she fell in love with him and gave him her hand in marriage. With his beautiful smile, black hair and soulful brown eyes he was strikingly handsome. As a child, brought up in a strict home, he was starved for fun, and so he loved her readiness to laugh and have a good time. The envious whispers of the others persisted to this day.

"She married Claude, an important man with wealth!" they said.

Only their children, and the family's housekeeper Annie, knew that he was not good to her. To others he was a man to be envied and idolized. No one knew that his family feared him.

But all disquieting thoughts were crowded out of the children's minds today because Robert and Theresa were consumed with the news of the picnic! They counted the days as they went by and with each day their excitement grew until, at last, the day had come.

Their family's horse-drawn carriage rode in the open air as it traveled to Timber Lake. The children took in all the sights and sounds of the journey from the back seat. First, they sat like little ladies and gentlemen as they rode through the streets of the town. All the small shops were closed. Everyone was going to the picnic! Then, once out on the open dirt road, they got onto their knees and faced backwards watching the town grow small behind them. It faded into the distance as small farms began to appear. They made a game of counting the cows and horses they passed. After the farms disappeared there were only meadows full of wildflowers, swaying in the breeze from the passing carriage. Then, as they turned to face the front, their laughter stopped. Their eyes grew large as they saw before them a huge, primeval forest.

The sight of the tall trees, as far as the eye could see, dumbfounded them! The sunlight changed to hazy shafts as they entered the forest, and the sweet musky scent of the trees made them giddy. As the carriage horses carried them deeper into the woods the smell of the living lake filled the air. They could smell the fish, the soaked wood and seaweed. It was thrilling to them. A little further in they could smell the food cooking in the barbecue pits and hear the distant laughter of the crowd.

Not able to control their excitement they leapt from the carriage as soon as it stopped at the entrance to the picnic grounds. They could see Timber Lake in the distance, through the woods, and the bobbing wooden raft at its center. They knew their mother had brought their swimming suits so they could swim later that afternoon when it got hotter. They ran through the crowd of happy, friendly employees and townspeople as a brightly uniformed band played polkas and waltzes. They went up to a table draped in festive fabric and multicolored paper garlands.

"Can we have two hot dogs please?" Robert asked breathlessly.

"Of course you can young man," the smiling lady behind the table answered.

"See, I told you!" Robert said gleefully to his admiring little sister.

They went from table to table eating everything their hearts desired. And it was all the best they had ever tasted. As they happily ate two ears of roasted corn dripping with butter, they saw groups of workers surrounding their father, vying for his attention. Some were talking very respectfully to him, others trying to make him laugh. He was an important man. Everyone wanted to be his friend.

Robert, at six years of age had formulated some thoughts about their father but didn't dare put them into words. He knew that his father adored him. He took great pride in that Robert looked just like him, with brown eyes and thick black hair. His father treated him like a prince. Robert knew he had nothing to fear. But he saw how his father treated his mother and sister. Without knowing the name for it, Robert longed to be their "protector".

Food was enjoyed, and laughter, dancing and games were everywhere. The sun was high in the sky, and it was hotter than before. It was time to go swimming. It was the best day of Robert and Theresa's lives.

Their mother took them to the bathhouse, a curtained wooden wagon on wheels near the shore. Piled beside it were large, shiny black inner tubes that were used to float on the lake. They saw women and children playing in the water, with ropes, anchored to the bathhouse, tied around their waists to protect them from being swept too far out by the powerful currents. They climbed into the wagon and Greta helped them to change into their swimming suits. Much to their surprise their father was waiting for them when they came out

"Come on Robert," he said. "Let's swim out to the raft. "

Robert was a good swimmer, but Theresa had not yet learned to swim.

"What about Theresa?" Robert asked.

"She can hang on to my back," their father replied.

The children tried to hide their discomfort with this idea.

"Wait for me to change," he continued. "I'll be right out".

Theresa hung onto her father's neck as he swam. She was frightened. He was a very powerful swimmer. She could feel his strength. Despite her fear the ride was fun, except for the occasional swallowing of water that slapped against her face. Theresa's father's strong arms lifted her up onto a short ladder attached to the side of the old, waterlogged raft, and then steadied her against its bobbing motion. She climbed onto its splintered surface. She watched Robert climb onto the raft by himself and marveled that he could do anything. Then her father, looking like a god, climbed onto the raft in one swift motion. At that moment she loved him very much. The three of them sat there soaking wet and laughing, on the bobbing raft in the bright sunshine, in the middle of the lake, looking at the towering green trees, listening to the distant laughter and music of the picnickers on the gaily decorated shore. She remembered her brother's words, "It's just like heaven". They sat contently for a while.

Then her father turned to her and said, "It's time you learned how to swim."

Her body seized with tension, and she felt a panic that muddled her breathing, Robert tried to hide his fear.

"Come on," her father continued, "I'm going to teach you how."

Theresa said nothing. She didn't talk around her father because when she did, she became confused and stuttered and lisped. She had stopped talking to him because he would play tricks on her. Tell her things weren't there that were there. He would tell her she was the idiot daughter of an idiot mother. She didn't want him to teach her how to swim but she dared not tell him. He pulled her to her feet and turned her to the side of the raft looking away from the shore. The side of the raft where the water was deeper, and the current was stronger: the side where no one could see her from the shore. He picked her up and threw her into the water.

The velocity with which he threw her sent her plunging deep beneath the surface. She opened her eyes and saw fish passively gliding past her, carried by the current. She struggled upward with desperate slapping motions, then tried to keep her head above the water. She went under again. This time she didn't go down as far. Trying to hold her breath, she again waved her arms wildly attempting to reach the sunlight that defined the surface. As her head appeared above the water she tried to scream and gasp for air, but she choked as the water filled her mouth. She saw Robert frantically pacing up and down with a look of horror on his face. She saw her father sitting on the edge of the raft, unnaturally still, dangling his feet in the water. Sure that he must not see her she struggled to make eye contact with him. But when she did, his eyes were not human. They were a staring, empty void. She burned with shame. She had done this to him. This was her fault. Everyone knew that her father was good. She had done something wrong. She desperately wanted to tell him that she was sorry. She went under again. This time things he had said and done flashed quickly before her.

"Some children should be drowned at birth, like unwanted kittens," he had screamed at her mother as he pointed to her.

"There isn't any cake," he told her, as her birthday cake sat in clear sight on the table.

"Why did you tell me that," she asked.

"Because I wanted to hurt you," he coldly answered.

"You don't deserve any dolls because you are a terrible mother," he said as he came upon her singing to her doll.

Her tongue would become so tense that she couldn't talk. Or it would writhe in confusion in her mouth not wanting to say something wrong. At these times she would forget how to breathe.

"You're an embarrassment," he would tell her when she would stutter or lisp, too confused and frightened to think straight. "You're the idiot daughter of an idiot mother. "

She couldn't see where the sunlight was anymore and she began to sink, as if being swallowed up by the lake. Everything slowed down and she was lost in shadows. She was going to sleep. In her mind's eye she saw her mother crying and reaching out to her. And then there was only the shadow of her mother left.

Unexpectedly she felt two small hands under her arms. It was Robert. The little boy used all the might in his six-year-old body to fight against the current and pull her to the surface of the water. He had dived in despite his father's order not to.

"She has to learn on her own," he had told him.

Their father sat motionless as Robert, confused and courageous, struggled to swim back to the raft with one small arm while using the other to hold Theresa's dazed body close to his. She could feel his heart pounding hard from the effort, and in the coldness of the water she could feel the warmth of his tears on her face. He pushed and pulled her up the small ladder onto the raft. Theresa lay there coughing up water as Robert gasped for air. Her only thoughts were of terrified drowning kittens, and she began to scream...a silent scream that wouldn't stop ripping through her, turning her small being into chaos. The two lay there, exhausted and breathing hard.

After a while their father looked at them with a blank face and said, "She'll never learn how to swim that way." Then he broke out into a loud laugh.

Some of the other children had thrown the big shiny, black inner tubes into the water and were floating on them to the raft.

"You can get a ride back to shore with those children," their father said. Then he dove off the raft and swam away with strong even strokes.

As the happy rambunctious children climbed onto the raft Theresa and Robert felt profound relief. Robert started playing with the other children as they made a game of jumping into the center of the big inner tubes. Theresa, belying her inner chaos, sat there, very quietly. Everything was different. There was no color. The trees, the water, the raft, the children, the picnickers and the banners on the shore, all that had been brightly colored before was now black and white. The sound of the children laughing and the music from the picnic was far away. She could barely hear it. She had gone far away. She was awake but in a deep sleep.

When the coolness of evening raised goose bumps on the children's wet skin, they all climbed back onto the inner tubes and floated back to shore. Robert and Theresa's mother greeted them with hugs and dried them off with big warm towels. She dressed them in the sweaters she had brought along. She was a loving and thoughtful mother. Their father walked over, no longer still and empty, but a happy charming man surrounded by admirers.

"I tried to teach Theresa how to swim," he told their mother.

"How did she do?" their mother asked with a smile.

"Not too bad," he said. "She'll do better next time."

Theresa and Robert stiffened with fear as his admirers laughed.

In the remaining hours of the picnic more food was eaten, and more games played. Robert joined in but Theresa couldn't concentrate to even know what the games were. She stayed at her mother's side. Then, in the moonlight, there was dancing. Everyone's eyes were on Claude as he danced with his stunning wife Greta, and they all thought them to be the happiest, luckiest people on earth.

On the way home Theresa sat very still in the carriage. Her mother looked at her and said, "You're all tired out."

Theresa said nothing. Robert looked at her anxiously. He knew. He was the only one who would ever know.

The rest of the summer was a blur to Theresa. Her father, Claude, went away to Europe for business. This provided her with a degree of calm. Life went on as usual, but she was absent. She was far away in a black and white world made of lines and the spaces in between them. The space in between the lines was where her soul, barely clinging to her body, rested. She inhabited that space, outside of her body. She learned that it was here, where the light was, that defined her, and not the solid lines. Many years later she learned that this was called the "negative space". But now she only knew this space as her refuge. There was no screaming there, only silence. When the light was diminished the shadows came. Then the screaming started. At those times she fled into the calm silent darkness where no one could find her.

It was during these times of isolation that Theresa began to draw. Her mother had art supplies on hand for the children, and now Theresa put them to use. She only used the lead pencils and the drawing paper. She would sharpen the pencils to a very fine point. The solid lines mustn't be too thick. Then, with a soft sensitive touch, she drew the spaces between the lines. As she drew, she felt that her hand was guided, maybe by the hand of God.

Every Sunday Greta took Theresa and Robert to church. Dressed in their finest clothes their whole community would attend services to worship together. It was while sitting in church, bathed in Sunday prayer, that Greta began to see color again. She awakened from her deep sleep to see tiny pinpoints of colored light, a little at a time, fields of tiny dots of color, smaller than the point of a needle. They were never a solid field. No matter how close together they were she could always see the white light behind them. Every Sunday there were more fields of them, filling up her vision. Slowly she began to see the pinpoints of colored light every day. The sky was turning blue again, the grass, green. But nothing was as before. Now they were always made up of the tiny points of color. And always the white light behind them was bleeding through. Even when she saw color consistently again, it was always in this way. At times it seemed that the light was the grace of God shining brightly through the pinpoints of its created images. At other times it seemed as if the light was trapped and trying to escape. But over time she forgot that this was not as it had always been. She accepted it.

3

Robert was distraught as he watched his sister become so strangely silent and withdrawn.

Their mother had said: "It's just part of growing up," and didn't think much of her behavior. He kept Theresa company as much as he could. They would go for walks, play marbles and sometimes he would read his favorite book to her: *King Arthur and His Knights of the Round Table*.

"This is the time of Arthur, and we will reach for the stars," he read to her. These words stirred her and opened her frightened heart.

He was a nice young boy with lots of friends to play with in these midsummer days, but he was always preoccupied with worry when he left his sister alone. He had trouble falling asleep at night. He would feel himself growing very small and then growing very big. He would wake up in the morning overwhelmed with anxiety. Then he would remember that his father was far away, and he would feel better. He would thank God that his father, who adored him, wasn't there. This was his guilty secret.

The summer was coming to an end now. Robert was turning seven and would soon be going back to school. He would be in the second grade. Greta planned a birthday party inviting all of Robert's friends and their families as well as Pastor Theodore and the family physician.

The day of the party, the large, balloon-festooned house was filled with good will and fun. The boys played kick ball on the expanse of green lawn in front of the long, bannistered porch, where the older guests congregated to enjoy the refreshments served by Annie, Greta's Irish housekeeper. Theresa stayed silent and at her mother's side as she graciously made everyone feel welcome.

Greta was at her best in a situation like this. Her stunning beauty and lovely smile made others feel at home. Her fun loving, flighty chatter was just right for a party atmosphere. And her housekeeper Annie's lilting Irish accent, twinkling blue eyes and abundant red hair added to the festive mood as she attended to the guests. In the late afternoon Happy Birthday was sung, and Robert cut his big, beautiful cake. The adults ate the cake while the boys chased each other, and laughing hysterically, smashed it into one another's faces.

A messenger arrived with a telegram and a big box for Robert. It was a birthday surprise from his father. As Greta cut a piece of cake for the messenger, she called out to Robert to come and open his present. Robert arrived on the porch panting and covered in frosting and cake crumbs.

"You open it for me," Robert said laughingly as he showed her his hands.

The guests all gathered around the porch. Inside the box there was a large book. Greta opened it to reveal photographs of uniformed soldiers carrying rifles, with swords at their sides. She held it up for all to see. Robert was immediately fascinated. Under the book was a folded military uniform. It was the uniform of a cadet. Robert was riveted. Greta put down the book and turned the box on its side so their guests could see the uniform.

"Read the telegram please," Robert implored her. She read the telegram loudly so all could hear.

"My Dear Son, for your birthday I give you a future filled with opportunity and good fortune. I have secured a position for you at a prestigious elementary Military Academy for boys aged seven to twelve. It is a very fine school where you will learn to be a soldier. More information when I see you. Happy Birthday from your proud Father. "

There was a respectful silence and then the crowd burst into cheers and applause. Robert felt like he had been struck by lightning. This was the answer to his prayers. This was the solution to all his troubles.

"I want to try it on," Robert exclaimed excitedly as he reached for the uniform.

"Not until you wash your face and hands," his mother proclaimed as she slapped his frosting covered hands away.

Everyone laughed, and Robert did too.

"I'll be right back," he shouted to the crowd as he raced up the stairs to wash in the basin in his room.

Pastor Theodore assisted him, picking up the gift box and following behind. Theresa followed too. The Pastor put the box on the bed while Robert washed, and was leaving just as Theresa was entering.

As Robert dried his hands he said to her, with a newfound confidence, "You don't have to be afraid anymore. I'm going to be a soldier with a sword and a rifle. If father tries to hurt you or mother, I will take him prisoner and lock him up. He will never hurt you again. I can protect you now". He reflected for a moment, then continued, "I will warn him, but only once".

"Will you warn him about the k . . .kittens?" Theresa asked with great concern.

"Yes"! Robert answered as a tear came to his eye. Then Robert's voice lowered and he leaned in close to his sister. "Theresa," he said, "before I leave I am going to teach you how to swim".

Theresa trusted him. For the first time since Timber Lake the silent scream grew fainter, and she began to feel happy. She left the room so Robert could change.

When Robert rejoined the guests, in full uniform, everyone gasped. He was no longer the carefree boy covered in frosting and crumbs who ran out of the room just minutes before, but a splendid young man, confident, serious, with a purpose. He had found his identity. This image of Robert was forever emblazoned upon Theresa's mind.

In two weeks their father was coming home to accompany Robert to military school. He planned to stay near the school in a hotel for several days, as many of the parents did, to attend the school's greeting ceremonies and orientations. Then he would return to Europe immediately to oversee the construction of a new warehouse. So in these two remaining weeks of their togetherness, Robert taught Theresa how to swim.

They started on dry land. As they stood on the lawn, he showed her how to move her arms and make cups of her hands to move the water. He showed her how to move her head in coordination with her arms to breathe in when her head was out of the water, and out as she exhaled into the water. Once she had conquered this, they moved to their oversized claw foot bathtub, filled with water. Dressed in her swimming suit, he had her practice only her breathing first. When she was good at that he showed her how to hold onto the back of the tub and kick her legs in coordination with her breathing. This process took a week. Theresa was a good student. She trusted Robert and would do anything he said. Now the moment of truth had come. Early in the morning, they put on their swimming suits and headed down to a small, nearby swimming hole.

As they waded into the cold water Robert said with great authority, "First I'll hold you up until you get used to being in the water. And then when you have a feel for it," he continued, "I'll let you go. But I'll stay right beside you so you don't have to be afraid," he assured her.

Theresa wasn't afraid. She was excited. This was her emancipation from victimhood.

When they were waist deep in the water, she took a deep breath and laid across Robert's extended forearms. At first it was hard to coordinate all the elements he had taught her, especially keeping a smooth flowing breath. But after only a few minutes everything started working together and Robert lowered his arms. Theresa remained buoyant and moved forward in the water with Robert beside her at the ready. Overexcited she lost her breathing coordination and started to panic. But Robert was right there to hold her up. They repeated this for almost an hour, and then after a brief rest they began again. This time Theresa's muscles had learned what to do. She only had to concentrate on keeping her breathing smooth and in sync with her body. She and Robert worked on this together. Several hours later she was swimming impressive distances on her own.

"You did it Theresa," Robert said in solemn congratulations. "You're a good swimmer."

He had fulfilled his first intentional duty as a "protector." He knew the word now: "Protector." Theresa, with her brother's help, had taken her first step to freedom. She knew for the first time how it felt to be capable. They went swimming every day until the day he left.

"You have to build up your strength," he warned her. "So if you ever get caught in a strong current," they both took a deep breath to fight off tears, "you'll be strong enough to save yourself."

Only Robert knew what had happened to Theresa. Only Robert could have saved her. They were a fortress unto themselves.

4

Ever since the day Robert had made his entrance into the party as a cadet, Theresa had been creating drawings of him. She had made many drawings over the summer that she kept hidden. They were documentations of her black and white world of exile and shame, and of her home between the lines. But the drawings of Robert were different. They were created with love and devotion. Her drawings of him became more and more accomplished. For the first time she wanted to share her secret world. She decided to give the very best one she could create to Robert as a going away gift.

The night before their father was to take him away, Theresa, with the drawing in hand, knocked on the door to her brother's room.

"Come in," said Robert.

He was already packed and sat intently reading his military book. He had worked on memorizing every infantry's motto, rules, regulations and traditions until they became ingrained in his mind. He wanted them to be second nature. As he lowered his book Theresa extended the drawing she had made of him. He was stunned at the sight of it. She had drawn him standing at attention in full uniform with his sword at his side.

"Did you draw this?" he asked in amazement.

"Yes," she replied shyly. "A p...present for you." She barely stuttered around Robert.

It was a remarkable likeness, but captured more than that. Her light touch and fine lines created a portrait of him that seemed to be floating on the paper. The fine lines didn't diminish the details but made them more present and important. His countenance and bearing were strong but also sensitive and filled with light. He looked like the noble spirit that he imagined King Arthur to be. So much so that he whispered King Arthur's words as they raced through his mind.

"We are civilized, resolved, and we will live through this together, Excalibur, they, you and I, and may God have mercy on us."

Then he jumped up and proclaimed, "It is so good! It is so good! We must show mother. We must show everyone!"

Theresa had a moment of fear, but then in an instant knew that the time had come to shed this fear and be happy again. As she ran down the stairs behind Robert, the silent scream loosened its grip on her and retreated. She was able to lock it away.

He excitedly cried out "Mother! Come see what Theresa has done!"

Greta was equally taken aback at what she saw. She looked at Theresa in awe. "We must frame this," she declared. "So Robert can hang it on his wall at military school!"

She gave the portrait to Annie, who got right to work on framing it so it would be ready by the next morning. They all fell asleep happy and at peace that night, mutually inspired and feeling so much love for one another.

Their father arrived early the next morning. Theresa was still asleep when he and Robert ate breakfast together. A breakfast filled with praise and admiration from Claude for his son

When Theresa came downstairs Robert was fully dressed in his cadet uniform. Their father was bursting with pride at Robert's natural military bearing and newfound maturity. Several family friends had come over to see Robert off. They stood in the large vestibule minutes before Robert and Claude had to leave to catch their train.

Pastor Theodore commented, "Claude, your son seems to be born to be a soldier." The others murmured in agreement.

Robert said unexpectedly "I have devoted my life to protecting the helpless and to confronting and fighting tyranny in all its forms." All murmured approvingly.

"That is a very serious mission," Pastor Theodore challenged, "Where will you begin?"

"As all must begin," Robert answered confidently, "At home."

As the Pastor nodded his approval Robert continued, "If any person were to harm my mother or my sister, it would be my duty to protect them." There was a slight chuckle among the men.

"And how would you protect them?" the doctor asked.

"I would take the offender prisoner," Robert replied.

"And what if he would not cooperate," his father challenged him with a smile.

Robert looked directly into his father's amused eyes and with stone cold certainty replied, "I would execute him."

No one spoke. For a fraction of a second Robert and Theresa saw, in their father's eyes, the still and empty man from the raft. But then he was gone in a flicker. No one else saw him.

The pastor broke the silence. "Such a commanding presence in one so young. Such determination!" He looked at Claude and continued, "Your son will be a man of consequence."

"He will be a great commander someday," the doctor added. "You must be very proud of him Claude. He is extraordinary."

This had shaken Claude to his core, but he managed to say, "I am very proud. Very proud."

The sound of the horses neighing outside broke the intensity of the moment and they knew that the carriage was waiting. It was time to go.

"One more thing father," Robert said, stopping everyone in their tracks. Looking directly into Claude's now questioning eyes Robert said, "I taught Theresa how to swim," he paused to see Claude's reaction. It was subtle but it was one of alarm.

"She worked very hard and learned very quickly. She deserves a reward. So, with mother's permission, I got her a kitten as a going away gift."

Annie bought out a basket with a tiny gray kitten in it. Everyone laughed with delight. Theresa was so surprised that she didn't know what to do. She lifted the fragile little creature from the basket and held it to her heart. She looked at her brother glowing with joy.

Robert continued, "A gray kitten to match Theresa's eyes." Then again, he spoke directly to Claude. "She will take good care of her kitten and no harm will ever come to it, as no harm should ever come to any innocent creature."

Claude looked confused.

Turning his attention to his sister, Robert asked, "What will you name your kitten Theresa?"

Without hesitation or a stutter Theresa exclaimed "Merlin!" All laughed.

Now Greta spoke. "Theresa has a going away gift for her brother." She nodded to Annie who handed her the portrait of Robert. Greta turned it around and held it high so that all could see. All were deeply moved by this unique and exquisite portrait that had been done by such a young artist. Especially Claude.

"Claude!" Pastor Theodore exclaimed, "You have two extraordinary children!"

"This is incredible," said the doctor, "Really outstanding."

"Theresa," Claude began incredulously, "I had no idea . . ."

Theresa didn't look at him.

Robert broke the silence as he moved forward to accept his gift. He kissed his mother on the cheek as she handed it to him. Then he turned and looked deep into his sister's eyes. Holding the portrait he whispered to her, "I will hang it on my wall in a place of honor. I will always be your protector."

He then turned and walked out of the door to the waiting carriage with great dignity. His father followed behind.

Everyone was very moved by these few minutes, most of all Claude. He had seen himself through his son's eyes. All at once the crushing weight of what his son had borne witness to, at his hands, came upon him.

"What have I done? What have I done?" The phrase repeated in his thunderstruck mind.

Robert and his father didn't speak in the carriage as they rode to the train station. The sound of the horse's hoofs on the cobblestones provided a rhythm that marked the passage of time while they sat in separate worlds thinking about their lives. Robert thought about his future as a soldier, and Claude about his past. The awareness that his son, at seven years of age, had the courage to stand up to him to protect his sister and mother had opened a door in Claude's unconscious mind that had been shut tight since childhood. No one had ever protected him. Nor had he ever had the courage to do what his son had done.

He had lived with his grandparents in the same house he lived in now, in the same small Wisconsin town. His grandfather, Charles, had been meticulously trained in the art of clock making since his childhood in Germany. He was a master. He was tall, blonde, with a lean muscular body and piercing blue eyes. His features were so finely chiseled that he looked like he had been carved out of stone by an exquisitely skilled sculptor. Most people thought him to be the handsomest man they had ever seen. As a young newly married man with a baby girl, he had come to the town where he began a business making and selling his clocks to shops in nearby towns and cities. He was a perfectionist with no tolerance for any deviation from perfection. He expected people to be like clocks, working in precise and impeccable order at all times.

As his business flourished, he expanded into making carved furniture. The quality of his work became known and eventually he was selling his products to dry goods stores around the United States. As the demand for his products grew, he began importing carved furniture from the Black Forest of Germany. He knew other craftsmen there who were of his caliber when it came to carving furniture, but no one was his equal in making clocks. Only he could deliver the level of excellence his clocks were renowned for. With the advent of Aaron Montgomery Ward's new mail order catalog his business grew so quickly that he had to hire young apprentices, that he deemed trainable, to assist him with the lesser functions of his work.

His daughter, Alice, fell in love with one such apprentice. He was a warm-hearted Italian boy from Sardinia. His name was Paolo. She, an isolated and lonely young girl, clung to Paolo for his acceptance and understanding. He wanted to give her all the affection that she had been deprived of. They fell in love. She became pregnant with his child. They went to Charles asking his permission to marry. Charles's answer was to beat the sixteen-year-old boy senseless, blinding him in one eye and breaking the bones in his hands so he could never work as an artisan again. He then drove him deep into the woods where he threw him from the carriage to the forest floor leaving him to die. He was never seen in the town again. It was a closely guarded secret that his fellow apprentices rescued him and hid him away while he recovered. They found a way to get him to New York where he had friends. From there Paolo told them he would work his way back home to Sardinia. With his gnarled hands he could no longer make a living as an artesian, but he could hoist nets. He would become a fisherman.

When Alice gave birth, her baby boy was taken from her to be raised by its grandparents. They named him Claude. Although only fifteen, she was forced to leave town. Claude never knew where she had gone or why she had never come back for him. She must have known how violent her father was, and yet she left him at the mercy of this cruel old man.

The steady sound of the galloping of the horses turned the stream of memories into a torrent. Claude couldn't stop them. They flooded over him, drowning his will.

He was only five years old when Charles took him away from his grandmother, Marzanna, and the beatings began. He would punish him for any fun-loving prank or high-spirited behavior. Sometimes he beat him simply because he had warm laughing brown eyes like his father Paolo. He would beat him mercilessly, while his grandmother looked on silently, too terrified to defy her husband. Then he was ordered to kneel and ask God for forgiveness.

As he got older the beatings got worse. The old man would drag him to the stable where he kept a noose for special punishment. He would put it around Claude's neck, and then throw it over a ceiling beam. He'd physically hoist him up off the ground, berating him while watching him choke, suffocate and flail. Claude would feel his heart pounding, harder and louder until his whole body was one deafening heartbeat, pounding so hard that it punched a hole in the sky. Finally, when Claude was almost unconscious, the old man would let go of the rope letting him fall to the ground. Then he would leave him to lie in the dirt, his soul saturated with the poison of hatred. Gasping for air he would look up at the ragged sky, as the hysterical horses kicked the inside of their stalls, while snorting and making horrible rattling sounds. As he lie there, the child in him separated from his body and locked itself away. He would not let the child be destroyed. He hid him far away.

His grandmother could see everything from the kitchen window, but she did nothing. She would turn a blind eye to him when, hours later, he'd stagger into the house, find his way to his room, then collapse on his bed for a night of fitful sleep.

Marzanna was tall and blonde like his grandfather. She was an orphan who had been taken in by a family to be raised as a servant. They did not regard her as anything more than a beast of burden. As a child, the only touch she knew was that of her bed, when exhausted and unloved she would roll back and forth on it, trying to comfort herself. Her small hands would reach out, grasping at nothing, imagining that one day they would find something to hold onto.

She was a beautiful young girl of fourteen when Charles laid eyes upon her. In his steady gaze she knew, for the first time, what it meant to be seen. When he asked the family for her hand in marriage she knew joy, also for the first time. Although he was ten years older than her, Marzanna was very much in love with him. His brilliance and good looks made him seem like a god to her. As soon as they married Charles began to discipline her to know her place as his wife. He admonished her for her hunger for him and delight at his touch. She became passive and dutiful, instead of natural and happy. He demanded that she hide her beauty, calling it modesty. He demanded that she not show her feelings, and to not speak unless addressed by him. She wanted with all her heart to please him, but gaining his love was like running up a hill that kept crumbling beneath her feet. Eventually she slid downhill into silent obedience and servitude. He had broken her already fractured spirit. Her beauty soon faded. She became Charles's shadow. Claude didn't know this. He blocked her out of his life along with any thoughts of his mother. But he couldn't block out his grandfather. His fear of him was so great that he too had been paralyzed into blind obedience.

One beautiful autumn day, when Claude was eleven years old, he came home from school to find the house unusually quiet. There was no smell of food cooking in the kitchen, no laundry hanging out to dry, or the bustle of chores being done. There was only an unaccustomed emptiness that hung eerily in the air. He knew that even though he had taken the path by the river, instead of the road, he wasn't late. He was never late. After carefully wiping his feet, he walked through the silent house, afraid that the sound of his footsteps might be too loud. He found his grandfather sitting, very still, at his desk, silent and staring out the window. Claude stood there and waited. He didn't speak. At home he never spoke unless spoken to.

"She's gone," Charles finally said with no emotion in his voice. "She's dead to us. We'll never speak of her again."

Claude remained silent. He couldn't risk a beating by asking a question. His first thought was that the old man had killed her. But he had never seen Charles direct his murderous rage towards Marzanna. And there was something in the old man's demeanor that was sad, even shocked, that she was gone. He never knew where she had gone and he never spoke of her again, nor did anyone in town. But it was whispered amongst the townspeople that she had been glimpsed, that same afternoon, on the road near the school. She was in a carriage, pulled off the side of the road, hidden in a clump of trees. She was with a woman who was wearing a veil. Some said the woman was her daughter Alice. The two were anxiously looking down the road, as if watching for someone. Some said it was Claude that they were waiting for, to take him away with them, but sadly he had taken the path by the river that afternoon. She was seen again shortly after that, seated on a train as it pulled out of the station. She was with the same veiled woman, and both women appeared to be crying.

After that afternoon, the punishments stopped. The old man trained him, not in clock making, but in business. He was to take over his import business.

Charles would say to Claude, "Your mother was no good. Your father was a libertine and a second-rate artisan. You were born of the sin of ungodly people. But I made a decent man of you."

Claude would reply, "Thank you Grandfather."

He never had the courage to stand up to him, or to even acknowledge to himself the truth of what their family life had been. He grew up sitting next to Charles in church every Sunday. His grandfather believed himself to be the perfect example of Christian values. No one dared to question this.

When Robert was born, Claude projected every good thing that he had locked away in himself onto his son. He could live a second childhood through him, with everything he ever wished for but never knew. He wanted to shower him with love, respect, guidance, opportunity and good fortune. He looked at his splendid boy, deep in thought, as the carriage moved along. He was in awe of him. Only Robert could have shown him the sick creature he had become. Only Robert, the boy he wanted to be, could have shown him this. He burned with shame and pain, but he didn't show it. He had learned long ago, never to show any feelings.

He could never lock his memories away again. Now they would forever be like a swinging lamp, exposed in the light then hidden in the darkness. They contained demons that were fighting for their lives. He had to grasp at them and examine them, no matter how they tried to hide from him. He had to destroy them and atone for his past if he was to have a relationship with his son, or ever face his wife and daughter again.

Once on the train, Claude engaged Robert in conversation about the military and was impressed at all that Robert had learned from the book he had given him. Robert was attentive. They passed the time constructively. Their relationship had changed. Claude was now being held prisoner within his son's cold uncompromising gaze. To his surprise he felt relieved and, somehow, he welcomed it.

The days that followed at the school were the most exciting of Robert's life. His unadulterated zeal flooded Claude with a happiness and pride that he had never known. But at night, alone in his room

Claude would weep. He would relive the horror of what he had done to Theresa at Timber Lake, telling himself that he was teaching her a lesson. Like his grandfather had done to him, he would have saved her at the last minute. This too, filled him with horror. He acknowledged for the first time what the acceptance of this sadistic behavior had done to him. He considered suicide. Maybe that would be best for everyone. He relived his verbal abuse of his learning-impaired wife, sweet and beautiful Greta, who loved him unconditionally. He paced the floor weeping until he would fall into a troubled sleep. But the next day at the school receptions and orientations, he would be charming and friendly. Nobody knew. Everyone wanted to be his friend. They thought Robert very lucky to have such a wonderful father.

When it was time for him to leave, he shook hands with Robert and in his unsmiling young eyes he saw a warning. He knew that Robert wasn't sad to see him go. He took a train to New York where he continued his journey to Europe on an ocean liner. He wept every night alone in his cabin.

5

Theresa loved her kitten, Merlin. She couldn't bear to be away from him. At night she took him to bed with her, but Merlin would go under the covers to wrestle with her feet wrapping his tiny body around them, shaking them and biting her toes. So Greta made him his own little bed in another room. Each morning, while still in her nightgown, Theresa would run to find Merlin who would greet her with purrs and head nudges, and they would spend the day together.

Theresa missed Robert terribly. She worked on her swimming to build up her strength, as he had instructed her to do. She practiced her arm work on the lawn while Merlin frolicked and pounced, and then in the bathtub, while Merlin sat watching her unblinkingly. She felt close to Robert when she practiced. Her breathing got smoother and deeper and more and more under her control. Theresa was very happy.

Several weeks had passed since Robert's departure when Theresa had a nightmare. She dreamed that her mouth had become a cage and a small, tortured white bird was caught inside. It writhed and beat against her teeth trying to escape. It wanted to fly away. She tried to open her mouth to let it out, but she couldn't. The silent scream was holding her mouth shut. She became more and more frenzied, twisting and turning her body trying to release the scream so the tortured bird could escape. She grew frantic knowing that if it didn't escape it was going to die. Then, in her dream, her brother appeared. He stood calmly before her showing her how to breathe. Mimicking him she took a deep breath, and her mouth opened in a piercing scream, releasing the little white bird from the cage of her mouth. It flew away swiftly. She screamed and screamed and screamed. Her Mother was awakened and rushed into Theresa's room to find her sitting up in bed, hysterical.

"Theresa!" Greta cried out. "Wake up! You're having a nightmare! Wake up!"

It wasn't until she was shaken that Theresa stopped screaming. She saw her mother and looked around her room before realizing that it had been a dream.

"You haven't had a nightmare like that since you started to talk, over two years ago. Do you remember?" her mother asked.

"No Mother," Theresa replied.

"You used to cry when I would try to put you to bed," her mother continued. "You didn't want me to leave your room. I would look under the bed and in the closet to show you that no one was there. And then I would sit with you until you fell asleep. But still, you would wake up in the middle of the night screaming, just like tonight. But now you don't even remember it. So you see, a bad dream can't hurt you. You'll forget all about it soon. I'll stay with you until you fall back to sleep. Everything will be fine in the morning."

Theresa lay back onto her soft pillow as her mother lovingly tucked her in. Even though Theresa had been terrified by the dream she somehow felt peaceful. As if a heavy burden had been lifted from her. The silent scream had broken free and been given a voice. Now it wasn't locked away. It was gone. The little tortured white bird was no longer writhing in her mouth but flying free.

Every week a letter would come from Robert asking how they were and telling them tales from Military School. He loved it there and was learning so much. They were wonderful letters. As her mother read them to her, Theresa would imagine her brother as young King Arthur about to pull the sword out of the stone.

On a Sunday afternoon, after the reading of one of Robert's letters, Theresa was at church praying. As she knelt with closed eyes and folded hands a white bird appeared to her. It was the same bird from her nightmare only now it was strong and healthy. With its wings fully extended it was sailing on the wind towards her. Then, in her vision, her mouth became a church with a high ceiling. Light was pouring in from the dome and all the windows. Then her tongue became the white bird. The tip of her tongue was the bird's head, the center of her tongue, its body, and the blades of her tongue its wings. The white bird wasn't trapped. It lived in this holy place. As the congregation stood to sing, she stood too but she did not open her eyes. To her mother's surprise Theresa began to sing.

The movement of her tongue as she pronounced the words made the wings of the bird rise and fall rhythmically as the center of her tongue, the bird's body, steadied and guided it. Powered by her breath the white bird took flight. Her song and the flight of the bird were one and the same. The domed ceiling of her church opened up to a limitless sky where the white bird soared, leaving all human conflict behind. It soared in a place of pure intention, where the invocation of sounds became a prayer.

If her eyes had been open, she would have seen that the congregation had all turned to look at her. Her pure and powerful voice was pitch perfect and filled with beauty. At the end of the song there was a hushed silence. All eyes were on her. The recessional hymn began to play, and the worshipers slowly left the church. In the vestibule the townspeople surrounded Theresa, showering her with praise, as Greta looked on, beaming with pride.

"You will be a famous singer one day," one said.

"You will be an opera star," said another.

"The Holy Spirit was speaking through you," one said with reverence.

"You have a very special daughter," a neighbor told her mother.

"You have an angel for a daughter," another said.

"She is beautiful inside and out like her mother," many of the kind neighbors murmured.

Theresa had never been called beautiful before and she wondered if it was true. She grew anxious to go home and look in the mirror to see what they meant. Eventually the excitement of the congregation quieted, and slowly everyone left to go home.

Theresa walked out of the church into the autumn afternoon. She could see the brilliant pinpoint colors of the changing leaves on the trees. She could feel the trees breathing for she was perfectly in tune with them. She, like them, was changing. She knew how to make the white bird fly. She wondered if that was what opera stars did. If they did, then she was one of them.

The only songs that Theresa knew were the ones she sang at church and a few Stephen Foster songs she heard the grown-ups sing at parties. Her favorite was *Beautiful Dreamer.* She had listened carefully and learned the words. She sang these songs constantly around the house. All day you could hear her singing, while she worked, while she played and when she just stood there doing nothing but singing.

When she had come home from church, on that first day the white bird had come to her, she looked in the mirror to see if she was beautiful. She wasn't sure if it was true, but she did become fascinated with looking at her reflection. She would stand in front of the mirror singing for hours with Merlin as her audience. He would look astonished and then roll around on her feet purring in adulation. She longed to learn more songs.

Unbeknownst to Theresa, a woman named Elizabeth had been

watching her. She was the choirmaster at church. She was a very dignified and poised woman, in her forties, never married, and childless. She had been a child prodigy and from a very young age had devoted herself to her career as a concert pianist and singer. She, accompanied by her mother, had performed all over Europe and the United States. When her mother died, Elizabeth was so grief stricken that she lost her ability to sing. No longer having the will to travel as a concert pianist she returned to her hometown in Wisconsin where she cared for her father until his death. She was very loved and respected by everyone in town. Elizabeth had noticed how Theresa stuttered and was unusually withdrawn in her father's presence. This concerned her. When she heard Theresa sing in church she was not only interested in her startling talent, but regarded this as the perfect opportunity to become involved in her life. One Sunday after church, she sought her out to compliment her on her beautiful voice and to invite her and Greta to her home.

When they arrived that evening Theresa was immediately fascinated by the beautiful grand piano in Elizabeth's parlor. Long ago, her grandfather Charles had made it. But Elizabeth didn't know that, and Theresa would never know. It was made of intricately carved wood and there were stacks of brightly colored sheet music covering its top.

"I want to learn more songs!" Theresa blurted out, unable to contain her excitement.

"Theresa," her mother began in a surprised tone. "Don't forget your manners!"

"I think it's wonderful that Theresa loves music so much," Elizabeth said to Greta. Then to Theresa she said warmly, "Please, come into the parlor and look through my music."

Elizabeth had a silver tray with lemonade, little cakes and tea waiting for them. She and Greta sat drinking tea and talking while watching Theresa hungrily pore through the stacks of sheet music. Everything about them excited her: the pictures on their covers of beautiful faces, charming gardens and singers standing in a spotlight. She loved the feel of the pages in her hands as she opened them and saw the cascading musical notes and written words called lyrics. She wanted to learn every song. She wanted to learn everything about music. She wanted to do nothing but sing in Elizabeth's parlor.

"Do you know any of those songs?" Elizabeth asked.

"I know *Beautiful Dreamer,*" Theresa replied. Elizabeth noticed that she did not stutter.

Elizabeth rose and went to the piano. "Would you like to sing it?" she asked.

Theresa was so excited she could only utter one word, "Yes!"

When Elizabeth sat down at the piano it seemed to Theresa that it woke up, as if it slumbered when Elizabeth was not near. As her fingers moved with graceful precision on the keys, the sounds moved through her whole being, warming her, moving her into a dance with the notes on the paper. They became music and filled the room with a sweet melody. She nodded to Theresa when she was to sing. Theresa closed her eyes and the white bird, eager to fly, was lifted into blissful flight.

Her mother sat very still, quite enraptured as her daughter sang:

Beautiful Dreamer, Wake unto me.
Starlight and dew drops are waiting for thee…

Greta felt a stirring inside herself as she, an audience of one, witnessed her daughter's first performance. It was as if doors inside her, that she hadn't known existed, were opening and filling her to the brim with joy. She could hardly believe that Theresa was her daughter.

This evening was the beginning of a relationship that would last throughout the rest of Theresa's childhood. Elizabeth taught her how to read music, play the piano, and strengthen her God given singing talent with breathing and vocal exercises.

Theresa's appetite to learn music was insatiable. She was singing opera arias by the time she was seven. Behind the piano there were bookshelves lined with large, bound books, containing volumes of sacred music and opera scores. These books were what Theresa wanted to study now. She wanted Elizabeth to help her to learn not only opera arias, but whole librettos.

"I'm going to be an opera star," she would tell Elizabeth and her mother".

"That is a very difficult life," Elizabeth would caution her. "You would have to learn Italian, French and German to be a professional opera singer. You can't learn an entire opera phonetically like you can an aria. You must speak the language. You would have to travel constantly from one opera house to another, and you must be very disciplined when it comes to taking care of your voice. Instead you could become a concert singer and sing popular music in English along with some of the well-known opera arias. That way you could have a more normal life. You could have a family and children when you grow up."

"I want to study the languages and sing what the opera composers wrote in those books," Theresa answered insistently, as she looked longingly at the shelves of musical scores. She and the white bird were now eager to go on extended flights through the soundscapes of the greatest music ever written. Even at her young age when she sang arias, she thrilled to feel the new languages on her tongue as she surged through their atmospheres.

"I want to be an opera star. That is what I want my life to be," Theresa repeated with certainty. "I already have a family. I don't want another one. I only want to sing."

Greta and Elizabeth worried that her childhood wasn't easy or happy. Except for her brother, Theresa didn't have friends as most children do. The other children didn't understand the tight focus she had learned in order to speak without a lisp or a stutter and they thought her stuck up because of her perfectly articulated speech. They ridiculed her behind her back, but because of her important father, they dared not attack her openly. She spent all of her time after school singing, studying and learning music, with Merlin as her only companion.

But Theresa wasn't unhappy: quite the opposite. She was exceptionally happy. She had found her purpose in life much earlier than others. She had left childish thoughts behind her on that autumn day when she first sang in church. Theresa was fortunate in that her parents could not only afford to hire tutors to teach her languages, but were willing to do so. And so she began to prepare for her career as an opera singer in earnest, at the age of seven, in the safe haven of her peers' underestimation of her.

6

Over the years Greta wrote to Claude regularly as he traveled throughout Europe expanding his business. When she first wrote to him about Theresa's talent for singing, the attention paid to her by the town, and her lessons with Elizabeth, Claude saw it as an opportunity for the atonement he so desperately sought.

He had acquired some exquisitely carved Pleyel pianos in France. He was importing them to New York but he would have one sent to his warehouse in Wisconsin to give to Theresa for her Christmas present. He always came home at Christmastime to be with his family. But this year, before returning home, Claude had formulated a plan. He was no longer in denial.

He had spent his evenings walking the streets of the cities of Europe, agonizing over his dangerous fits and brutal behavior. He knew that these dark spells were beyond his control. Like demons, they would spring forth unexpectedly, animating his body to do their vicious bidding. The world would suddenly become exaggerated, bright and vivid. The sky would become a powerful deafening whirlwind above him. The ground beneath him would churn, trying to swallow him up as he walked upon it, while the blades of grass became little sharp razors trying to cut his feet. The branches on the tress would reach out to maliciously slap and strangle him, while the leaves sought out his eyes to blind them. Everywhere he looked he would see evil intent. The people he knew and even loved would become possessed by it, tormenting him, trying to deceive and destroy him. Their bodies would change. They became animal-like and predatory. Their voices would change. He could hear the warped voices of demons speaking through them, lying to him, humiliating him and driving him to madness. He would strike out at the demons that came near him, to hurt them, humiliate them, and render them powerless. But now he was determined to remain perfectly still in the silent center of this monstrous force. It was his only defense.

So this Christmas, when his dark spells descended on him, he would immediately leave the house and seek out Pastor Theodore's help. He would not return home to his family until the spell passed. He promised himself that he would never harm his family ever again. If need be, he would harm himself instead.

That first Christmas was relatively happy for the family. Robert came home from his first semester at military school full of stories of his adventures. His family sat at rapt attention, filled with admiration as they listened to him.

Theresa sang *Silent Night* in church on Christmas Eve, which filled the family with pride and the entire congregation with abounding Christmas spirit. Father Theodore had asked her to do a portrait of the Holy Family, which now hung in the church's vestibule. The sensitivity of Theresa's images made the parishioners feel as if they had been transported to that cold stable, to stand under the star of Bethlehem in the presence of Mary, Joseph and the Infant Jesus.

On Christmas morning Claude presented his son with a horse, which Robert named Gwydion. It was the name given to King Arthur when, as an infant, he had been hidden away in Wales until he could safely assume the crown. Robert bonded with his horse instantly and went riding every day of his Christmas vacation, sometimes with his Father, and sometimes with Theresa seated behind him.

To her amazement, Claude presented Theresa with a piano. A Pleyel. The kind played by Chopin and Debussy, and which was memorialized in Renoir's painting *Woman at the Piano*. She immediately sat down and played a simple Bach tune that Elizabeth had taught her. Claude respectfully listened and to her surprise praised her.

In the weeks that followed he secretly stopped whatever he was doing to listen to her at the piano doing her daily vocal and piano exercises. He wanted to reach out to her but he couldn't. He was too ashamed.

He gave his wife a sapphire necklace purchased from Cartier in Paris. As he fastened it around her neck the children thought she looked to be the most beautiful woman on earth.

He gave Annie, their housekeeper, a strand of Mikimoto pearls and a generous bonus. The pearls made Annie's skin glow, and the bonus was greatly appreciated.

The usual tension was present, as it always dominated the home when Claude was there. But uncharacteristically, Claude said very little, preferring to listen. He was very grateful for the gifts given to him, and that his favorite foods, prepared by Greta and Annie, were served. He drank noticeably more than usual this year. Sometimes he would drink until he fell asleep. Several times he left the house hurriedly and did not come home for hours. It was these times that he found his way to the home of Pastor Theodore where he would pace and rage and tell him of his agony.

"You understand Pastor," he would rage with terrible intensity. "You know where we are. We are in Hell. This world is Hell, and we are all possessed of evil. It is always there, waiting to clutch at us and drag us down to violence and depravity."

He would then implore, "You are in a constant battle with evil. Show me how to keep it away. I have learned to live most of my life asleep, in a dream pretending to be someone else. But for these brief periods I wake up from my sleep and I see it all. I feel it all. When I am fully present, I am in Hell. I rise up and I am the devil himself. Help me brother." He sobbed. "Teach me how to pray. Show me how to survive this torture of being fully awake. Keep the demons from devouring me. Help me not to harm my family."

"We will find a way," Pastor Theodore would reassure him. "We will not despair," he continued. "To despair is to sin."

Then Pastor Theodore, a true holy man, would enter into Claude's safe place of stillness and pray with him for hours. Sometimes he would hold both his hands to transfer strength and grace to him. The repetition of the holy words seemed to subdue Claude as his hell spun around him out of control, until it finally subsided.

The years that followed were happier ones for the family. Theresa was working with tutors to learn the languages she had to know to become a classical singer. Robert was flourishing in Military School, Greta was no longer being humiliated and berated by her husband, and Claude was becoming a very wealthy and successful international importer. His spells still came upon him but he was able to manage them by removing himself when they struck.

When Robert came home in the summer, he and Theresa went swimming at the swimming hole. And although Decoration Day picnics at Timber Lake continued, Claude never asked to go swimming with his children again.

With the passage of the years the children's memories were occupied with other things. Their futures, once hidden inside them, were now unfolding day by day as they were consumed with learning. Long-term memories were relegated to the service of the present, while other memories, too destructive or painful to cope with, were locked away. Yet still they echoed in their minds, like a dissonant note of music, or a distant feeling of dread. But they no longer required constant vigilance.

The children had each found a quest, a way to break free from the terror of their past experiences. Greta was never able to hold onto memories unless they concerned her children's safety. She lovingly tended to her children and her husband, whom she loved deeply, and what she did remember was all happy. Only Claude remained prisoner to his memories and the deeply chiseled suffering they contained.

7

At sixteen Theresa was an accomplished singer with an impressive four-octave range and a notable repertoire. She could sing everything from Mahler to Mozart. Elizabeth arranged an audition for her with an opera impresario she had known and trusted. His name was Maximillian. He was going to be in Milwaukee to meet with Mr. Pabst, the owner of the Pabst Opera House. She and Theresa would take the early morning train to Milwaukee. Max had arranged for them to stay where he was staying, at The Pfister Hotel, described as "The Grand Hotel of the West". Theresa was anxious, but not afraid.

Like a thoroughbred horse she was ready to run, and straining at the bit to get on the professional stage. She had sung at church and at many town functions but had only seen pictures of the professional stages and opera houses where she was certain she belonged.

Theresa did not want to strain her voice by talking over the noise of the train: wheels chugging, whistles blowing and the passengers chatting, so she remained silent. Elizabeth no longer worried that Theresa was unhappy. She knew she was doing exactly what she wanted to do.

Max sent a chauffeured automobile to meet them at the train station. The sights on the drive to the hotel were thrilling, but Theresa barely noticed them. She was on a mission and would not allow anything to distract her. The hotel was lavish, luxurious and beyond any imagining. But Theresa couldn't enjoy anything until she was on the stage singing for Max.

Max had left a message for them at the hotel desk to meet him at the opera house. He was in meetings with Mr. Pabst but would be ready to hear Theresa sing mid-afternoon. He had no real expectations concerning Theresa. He was doing this as a courtesy to a fellow professional, Elizabeth, whom he knew and admired.

Once at the hotel Theresa didn't want to rest. She freshened up, tried to eat lunch, and was ready to go when finally it was time to leave. Upon arrival at the opera house Theresa barely noticed its grandeur. She only wanted to see the theatre and to be on its stage. The house manager, who had greeted them, led the way. He brought them down the various corridors and up the dimly lit stairways, which led to the surprisingly expansive stage. It was crowded with scenery for the upcoming opening night that was to occur next week. Others may have felt swallowed up by its enormity, but as Theresa stood there for the first time, she felt reverence and gratitude to finally have found her home. She never wanted to leave. She was eager to fill the space with her voice. Theresa walked to a piano that stood down stage center and arranged her music on the stand, eager to begin. She was ready.

Max entered in a flurry of attention from an entourage, all vying for his attention. He was powerful, sophisticated, and walked with the stature of an emperor. He greeted Elizabeth with the warm embrace of a true friend. When he turned his gaze to Theresa, she saw that he had very sad but kind eyes. His first impression of her was that she was not at all what he had expected. She was neither nervous, ingratiating, or over-confident. Nor did she have the usual affected manner of the inexperienced. She was still, focused and dignified beyond her years. There was no static to her being. She was as clear as a bell. She came to sing, not to be admired or encouraged. He liked her right away.

"How wonderful to meet you Theresa," he began. "I hope the trip did not tire you."

"Not at all," Theresa said, as she looked him directly in the eye. "I am ready to sing for you whenever you are ready."

Max was amused by her "no excuses" approach to their meeting and appreciated that she had no interest in wasting time. How he disliked those auditions where he was expected to get to know the young singer and make idle small talk to put them at ease. He knew everything he needed to know about any singer by hearing them sing.

"What have you prepared, Theresa?" He asked.

"I would like to sing, *O Mio Babbino Caro*, but I am prepared to sing anything you would like to hear", she answered. Max nodded with a slight smile. The pianist was seated and began to play the introduction. Finally Theresa was singing for Max.

As she began to sing Max observed immediately that there was no sentimentality or dramatics muddying up her beautiful tone, but a pure connection to what the composer wrote. The song sprang from her as though freshly conceived, brand new, a pure creation of the moment. Her emotional connection to the song was natural, nuanced, and free of contrivance. It was as if the song was singing her. Her lower range was rich and resonant, and her high range soared effortlessly, lighting up those listening with a radiance unreachable to them otherwise. He knew that she was very rare. He was captivated. He had her sing several other arias from the operas he was producing for his next season. She knew them all by heart and sang each one with haunting beauty, emotional maturity and artistic mastery. Max was already thinking of what roles to cast her in as he listened.

Her whole life changed that afternoon. Plans were made quickly. She would make her debut in Chicago as Mimi in *La Boheme*, and then she would play Lauretta in "*Gianni Schicchi*," in New York. He would give her the role of Cherubino in *The Marriage of Figaro*, and Juliet, in *Romeo and Juliet*, on tour with his company playing the many opera houses of Europe.

Theresa had only one question, "Can I bring my cat Merlin with me?"

Max understood. "Yes, if you like," he answered with kindness.

For Theresa working with Max was a dream come true. All during rehearsals he kept his eye on her as she eagerly experienced each step of the process for the first time. He saw how she loved to stand before the mirror, for costume fittings and make up sessions, looking at herself. Yet she wasn't admiring herself or preening. She seemed to be studying herself intently, as if surprised by a stranger looking back at her, or hungry for some fleeting wisdom or memory that lie in her reflection. She lived for her work. It seemed a matter of life and death to her. He wondered what had caused her to be so totally immersed in her art. He didn't know that singing had been her salvation from the tongue-tied stutterer she once was. He didn't know of the silent, black and white world she had lived in after Timber Lake. No one ever knew what had happened to her, except Robert.

Everyone could see the joy with which Theresa sang, but no one knew of the terror she felt at what would become of her if she should ever stop. She had never known how to live in the world that most inhabited.

When she sang, the emotional life of the music was so alive and compelling that everyone would stop what they were doing to listen to her. Max heard in her voice an elevation of pain to compassion that brought a tear to even his world-weary eye. Afterwards, as everyone applauded her, there was no conceit or entitlement, no self-satisfaction. She wasn't a diva. She was a vessel. Max had never seen this in one so young.

Her colleagues found that she wasn't friendly to them in the normal sense of the word, but that she was attentive and respectful to them professionally. They found that they did their best work when onstage with her. She was in her element. She had been born to be in the world of the opera.

Outside of rehearsals Theresa wasn't social at all. She spent her evenings in her room studying her roles, with Merlin purring at her feet. The only person she spent time with was Max. At his invitation she would eat her lunch and dinner with him. This might have caused alienation among the company members if they had not come to know her. But they had come to regard her as a valued friend. Besides, Max took good care of everyone in his company. They always stayed where he stayed, at the best hotels, and were often treated to celebratory dinners at the best restaurants. So even if there was a jealous remark about Max's attention to her, or rancor from a potential enemy, it never gained any traction, and those attacks were soon silenced.

Theresa's whole family, including Elizabeth and Annie, attended her debut in Chicago. It was Christmastime so they spent the holiday at the luxurious Palmer House Hotel, where the opera company was staying.

When Robert turned thirteen, he had transferred to St. John's Military School in Delafield, Wisconsin. He wanted to be close to home so he could visit often, especially when his father was there. He still felt the need to actively guard and protect Theresa and Greta against danger. But over time these feelings faded, for there had been no violent episodes. He excelled in school and won many marksmanship awards including that of "Distinguished Expert." When he turned eighteen, he was sought after as a sharpshooter by many prestigious schools. He chose instead to join the U.S Naval Academy.

He had traveled from The Academy in Annapolis, Maryland to attend Theresa's debut in Chicago. He was a strikingly handsome young man, especially in his uniform. His uncompromising gaze and military bearing were now second nature to him. Over time he thought less and less about their desperate origins. He turned heads everywhere he went. He was very proud of his sister and quite happily felt the magic of this Christmas.

Theresa's father had come back from Europe to be with his family for this monumental occasion. Claude was a very handsome man and looked every bit the successful businessman, dressed in his evening clothes alongside his beautiful wife Greta, radiant in the cream-colored Paris gown and ruby jewels that he had brought back from Europe for her.

Elizabeth wore a black velvet cape over a sapphire blue satin gown with simple diamond drop earrings, while Annie wore her pearls over a flowing pale green silk gown borrowed from Greta. Accompanied by Robert in his Annapolis dress uniform, they could not have been a more stunning group as they stood drinking champagne at the pre-show *soirée*.

Chimes sounded alerting the opening night audience that it was time to enter the theatre. The opera was about to begin. The audience murmured with excitement as they took their seats. It was a sold-out house.

Backstage everything was meticulously in place. The singers, the orchestra, the costumes, the sets, and the lighting: Max made sure that all were prepared and that all was perfection. The excited chatter of the audience turned to applause as the conductor made his entrance into the orchestra pit. Then there was an anticipatory hush as he raised his baton. Theresa embraced the hush, and felt cradled inside of it, as she waited in the wings. She listened intently for her cue to make her entrance. When it came, she stepped out of the quiet, and forward onto the stage. She could feel the audience. She could feel herself come fully alive before them as the doomed heroine Mimi.

Her opening notes resonated through the theatre, electrifying the audience. They became focused. She magnetically drew them to her, until they breathed with her. As their heartbeats synchronized to hers, they became one being. Then, in this transformed state, they soared with her into a rarefied atmosphere where ecstasy lived. They were with Theresa in the place of pure intention.

Afterwards there was a moment of disorientation as the audience returned from this breathtaking ride. For a few moments they were between two worlds. And then a tidal wave of love erupted, for her, for each other, for what they had just experienced. She was engulfed in a thunderous ovation.

It was a glorious Christmas for the family, despite the bittersweet realization that this was the end of a part of their lives. Both Robert and Theresa had left home to pursue their careers. Their parents were very proud of them, but at the same time their pride was tinged with sadness. Claude, realizing that his wife would be alone, now suggested that she accompany him on some of his trips to Europe. Greta was surprised and delighted at this new chapter in their marriage and in the success that had come into the lives of her children. Annie had a suitor and saw this as the perfect opportunity to marry him. Claude wanted them both to remain on as caretakers of the Wisconsin family home while he and Greta traveled. Elizabeth was humbled and gratified at the role she had played in Theresa's success. As a result of this relationship a healing had taken place in her heart and soul. In the last few years she had begun to sing again. It was very painful at first. Singing is an emotional art and, since her mother's death Elizabeth's predominant emotion was grief. For a long time she couldn't get through a song without breaking down in tears. Then unable to recover, she would give up in despair. But gradually, Theresa's joy and devotion helped Elizabeth to find those qualities in herself once more. She sang more and more until she was on top of her grief. Now she was ready to book concert tours again. This was a turning point for everyone. They had been battling not only each other, but themselves, for a long time. None of them had given up. And now they seemed to have come to a new season.

This was true of two other forgotten family members as well. In the very last row of the second balcony of the opera house, two shabbily-dressed women, Alice and Marzanna, sat, nervously clutching each other's hands. Although in the back row, they could not have been positioned more perfectly. They were among the most passionate of the opera lovers. Those who, like them, had scrimped and saved to afford a seat: the students, the artists, the singers, actors, dancers, musicians, writers, conductors, and the householders who knew every note of the score, sometimes quietly singing along. Marzanna and Alice had never been to the opera before. After escaping the tyranny of Charles, their lives had been spent in servitude, working long hours in a laundry, barely able to pay their way. Yet when the music began they felt a stirring deep inside. A longing that had patiently resided within them, silently, forbidden from acknowledgment or expression by the cruel domination of those who did not love them. But now the exhilaration of the orchestral music flooded their senses. It swept through their bodies as if God had taken them in his arms to dance. The shackles of shame, guilt, and confusion that had so mercilessly bound them, broke open and fell away. Fortified by the music their spirits rose, and like a wildflower bursting through a granite edifice, their hearts opened wide to receive the love that rained down on them in a symphony of acceptance and affirmation. They were fully engaged in every second of it. They applauded wildly, they cried, they laughed, they excitedly jumped to their feet crying out "Bravo" along with their devoted companions in the second balcony.

From their vantage point they looked out over the entire theatre, in awe, taking in the enraptured response of the audience members to their beloved Theresa. They were filled with wonder to know that she was their offspring. They were overcome with gratitude that they were present to witness this evening. Looking through their borrowed opera glasses they found Claude in the front row. Tears rolled down their cheeks as they watched him sitting next to his beautiful wife Greta, looking proud, handsome, regal, and very happy. At his other side sat his son, Robert, splendid in his naval uniform. He emanated such strength and goodness that they were in awe of him. The anguish of many years was washed away. They now felt pride and satisfaction in knowing that this family had been created through their bodies. Their offspring were well, happy and thriving, despite their inability to save them from the abuse and tragedies that they had suffered. This was the greatest gift these women could have ever been given. This was the greatest night of their lives. Afterwards, in their humble flat near the stockyards, they were truly happy. The memory of this evening would sustain them for the rest of their lives. There were never two more grateful and fulfilled women on this earth. This Christmas in Chicago would be forever held precious in the hearts of the entire family.

8

Max and Theresa were kindred spirits. They joined together like two drops of water at their very first meeting. It was not a romance. He was fifty years old and she sixteen. Their bond was in that they were inhabitants of the same world. They lived at the edge of the conscious mind in abstractions and exotic energy fields. They were not visitors there, like others, but permanent residents, consumed by the archetypes that live only in these remote regions. Their joy and purpose in life lie in experiencing and manifesting these intangibles, revealing something of the divinity that created them.

On the trains, steamships and ocean liners that took them around the world, when they weren't rehearsing, Max and Theresa would talk endlessly about composers and the intricate inventions of their compositions. They would talk about languages and compare the mastery of the different emotional soundscapes that they could capture and then encode effectively into words and music.

In the cities of Europe Max opened up the world of great masterpieces of art and architecture to Theresa. They roamed the great museums, galleries, cathedrals, gardens and piazzas together, of one mind, communicating effortlessly with a glance or a single utterance.

Theresa shared her sketches with Max, and he commented on her sensitive use of negative space. He encouraged her to pursue her art further and learn to paint. But she had no interest in anything beyond her sketches. He had no knowledge of how or why she began to draw. She told him that she only wanted to sing. He understood. Their companionship was a gift to both of them. When not working, they had both walked through the dream of life alone, observing it, and only tolerating it. Through their friendship they were now participating in it with open hearts.

Five happy years passed quickly, and Theresa was becoming a well-known opera star. At twenty-one she was a beauty with an hourglass figure, long dark hair and arresting gray eyes. She had learned to dress in fashionable clothes, as she was recognized wherever she went and sought out for photographs and interviews. Now when Theresa went swimming it was in a couture swimming costume on the Riviera, not at the swimming hole in Wisconsin.

Her repertoire had expanded to include adult roles. She had performed the leading characters in *Madam Butterfly*, *Aida*, and *Tristan und Isolde* to great acclaim. And now she was ready to make her debut as Violetta in *La Traviata* at the Palais Garnier Opera House in Paris.

It was March of 1918 and World War I was still being fought with the help of the Italian and the American troops. The war had not encroached upon the city itself, except for the presence of the Allied forces on the streets of Paris.

The Palais Garnier seated 1,900 patrons and had already sold out its opening night. To witness Theresa Berto, known for her purity, play the fallen woman Violetta opposite the irresistible Italian tenor, Salvatore DeCarlo, was the quest of every opera fan in Paris.

Max had heard Salvatore sing the role of Mario Cavaradossi in *Tosca* while in Rome. Not only did he have an extraordinary voice, but he was also strikingly handsome. He was young, tall, strong, with thick golden-brown hair and green eyes. He was pursued by women from all echelons of life. Aristocrats, heiresses, famous actresses, star-stuck young girls, opera aficionados: they all worshiped him. He was booked solid for two years, but undaunted, Max signed him two years in advance knowing him to be the perfect choice to play opposite Theresa, as Alfredo, Violetta's lover, in *La Traviata*. Salvatore had sung the role of Alfredo in Milan so it was in his repertoire, but it would be his first appearance at the Palais Garnier. After signing Salvatore, Max dedicated the next two years to preparing Theresa for what he instinctively knew would be a sensation.

Arrangements had been made for the company to stay at The Ritz Hotel, operated by Carl Ritz and his partner, famous French chef, Georges Auguste Escoffier. When it opened its doors in 1898 it quickly became renowned for its opulence, fine dining, and for being the first hotel to have electricity, a telephone, and a private bath in every room. Now, in 1918, it was a luxury hamlet for royalty and international travelers as well as the favorite haunt of the rich and famous.

As the company members excitedly unpacked their luggage and explored their luxurious accommodations, Theresa was instructed to leave immediately for a costume fitting. Max's car was waiting for her in front of the hotel in the cul-de-sac of the Place Vendome.

She was hurried into the tailor and alterations shop of the opera house. The shop mistress greeted her warmly as she brought her into a room humming with the activity of the designers, cutters, drapers and stitchers, all devotedly working at their craft. They all knew Theresa from her previous triumphs with them and they held her dear to their hearts. They were very inspired when creating costumes for her and always flourished artistically in their collaborations. They had taken great care to be sure that all of Theresa's costumes would be very special for her debut as Violetta. The mistress explained to Theresa that she had been searching for a fabric both unique and of incomparable beauty to use for the bodice of Violetta's ball gown for her duet with Alfredo. After an extensive search she had found an exquisite piece of antique fabric in perfect condition. As she produced the fabric Theresa's heart skipped a beat. It was a rich woven fabric made of gold, silver, and purple threads. Theresa knew she had never seen the fabric before, but somehow seeing it moved her deeply. She took it in her hands and ran her fingers over the threads. They seemed to speak to her. She spontaneously held it to her heart. Suddenly she missed someone terribly, but she didn't know who. The mistress, seeing her reaction was very pleased, thinking that Theresa appreciated the unique and breathtaking beauty of the fabric.

"I found it at an antique shop on the Left Bank near Notre Dame Cathedral," she began, enlivened by Theresa's response

"I was wandering around after church services and there it was in a basket with an old book of music. I asked the proprietor where they had come from, and he said a German peasant had brought them in a few weeks earlier. He had found them in the ruins of an old convent in the Black Forest outside of Mecklenburg. They were tucked away in a stone cupboard and had survived the years untouched. I have never seen such a rich weaving before. It must have been created by a master weaver for a very wealthy patron. No one does work like this anymore. I knew it was meant for you the moment I saw it," the shop mistress explained affectionately.

"I appreciate your finding this for me more than words can say," Theresa said as a tear rolled down her cheek.

The shop mistress got to work, diligently shaping and pinning the material in place as Theresa studied herself in the mirror. What was it about this fabric that moved her so deeply? What was she trying to remember? As she stood deep in thought the voice of a man filled the room. He was walking down the hallway singing a song. It was a haunting old religious song called *Salve Regina*. Theresa knew at once that she had never heard it before, and yet she felt as if she could anticipate every note as it was sung. The room came to a standstill listening to the man's voice, which was magical in its beauty. The man stopped singing as he entered the room. Theresa saw him reflected in the mirror she stood before. His eyes went directly to hers as he saw her reflection across from him. All was still. It was only a moment, but it seemed to go on endlessly, echoing through eternity.

Then, knowing that the silence must be broken, the man asked, "Is this the tailor and alterations shop?" His voice was rich and resonant.

"Yes, yes it is", the shop mistress stammered, breaking out of the spell he had cast.

"I am Salvatore DeCarlo." When he spoke it sounded like music. "I am here to be fitted for a costume."

As everyone broke free of their beguiled condition there were frenzied greetings, followed by a flurry of activity as he was led away to the tailor for his fitting. Once gone, his presence hung over the room like a blissful sigh. The others resumed their busy chatter but Theresa didn't speak. She was embraced by a scintillating silence. He had set everything in her being in motion.

Before Theresa left, she asked the shop mistress for the address of the antique shop where she had purchased the precious fabric. The mention of an old book of music called out to Theresa. She wanted to see the companion piece to the fabric that was contained in the basket, from the ruined German convent. She would have to wait until after opening night, but she made a mental note. She would go.

When she returned to The Ritz, she mentioned to no one that she had met the famous Italian tenor. She had worked with many talented male singers before, but this one was different. The others, however handsome, kind, and attentive, might as well have been in a different dimension. Although she was completely accessible and responsive to them on stage, they could not reach her personally. Many had tried. She had admirers among the talented, rich, and influential all over Europe, but had no interest in them or any time to give them, other than to politely succumb to a kiss on her hand. Her exclusivity inflamed their passions even more, but to no avail. Yet Salvatore, with one look reflected in a mirror, had penetrated her absolute ownership of herself. Her only other close relationships were with Max, Robert, and her mother. This was like none of them. This was a feeling unknown to her until today.

She put him out of her mind. She had work to do. She was disciplined. That night she stayed in her room rather than dining at Escoffier's restaurant with some of the others. She wanted to study her role and get a good night's sleep to be rested for rehearsal tomorrow. She worked for hours while Merlin happily rolled around at her feet purring. He had been fed scraps of fish from Escoffier's kitchen and was very content. Theresa was happy. She knew the role of Violetta by heart. She had performed other roles at the Palais Garnier and knew its stage and acoustics. She was prepared and well grounded to perform in the excitement and distractions of the first rehearsal with the whole cast.

When Salvatore returned to his room, he could not put Theresa out of his mind. He too had been impenetrable by the many who pursued him. But Theresa's reflection in the mirror had touched his heart and soul, stripping away the public persona of the famous tenor and leaving him vulnerable.

He was a troubled young man. He had a true vocation at an early age. He wanted to be a priest. At the age of seven he was accepted at the *Collegio Romano* in Rome. There he was quickly recognized for his devout connection to the sacred Liturgy of the Mass, and the ease with which he memorized and chanted it. He was regularly used as an altar boy. He was immersed in his studies until 1908, when shortly after his thirteenth birthday his father was crippled while working on the railway lines up in the Alpine region of Italy. A cart filled with heavy equipment toppled over, crushing his left side leaving him unable to walk or use his hand. His father, once the sustainer of their family, now sat in a chair unable even to fend for himself. So now Salvo had to leave the seminary. With frightened hearts, he, his five brothers and four sisters had to give up the life they had known and go to work.

Factories had opened up in their region of Italy, so the six boys got jobs there. The four girls got work cleaning cafes and washing dishes. It was confusing for the children, who had spent their childhoods depending on their families and extended families for their way of life. Now factories were plentiful, and the children once accustomed to surviving within the closeness of their families, were going in droves to work in them. There they learned to rely on cold and uncaring corporate bosses for their livelihoods. But the children were resilient. Salvo always sang as he worked, attracting the attention of all. Soon he was being asked to sing in cafes and for city celebrations. In time he found that he could earn more money singing at events than he made at the factory, and he could improve the life of his family.

It was four years later, at a civic event, that a director from an opera house in Milan heard Salvo sing and recruited him for his company. As most Europeans, Salvo spoke several languages. Since childhood he had learned very intricate sacred music at the seminary, so learning the operatic librettos and arias was not difficult for him. His angelic voice, devotional spirit and stunning good looks soon made him famous all over Italy. He made enough money to take care of his whole family now and would not allow them to work at menial labor anymore. He was very proud of this and for a few years all was well.

But in 1915 Italy became involved in World War I. All his brothers joined the Army. They felt duty-bound to follow in the footsteps of their grandfather, a war hero, who had lost his arm fighting alongside Garibaldi in his final, successful, 1870 War of Italian Unification and the creation of the Kingdom of Italy. Salvo was torn to know that his brothers were risking their lives fighting for their country while he was singing in grand opera houses and living a life of luxury. He wanted to serve as other men served, but his years of prayer in the seminary taught him to pray for peace and salvation. He did not think he could kill another man no matter what the cause.

"Yet," he pondered, "the archangel Michael battled Lucifer in heaven, so are not some battles ordained by God?"

But who would support his family if he did join the army? All these conflicting thoughts tormented him.

Meeting Theresa had soothed his soul. He felt he had stepped out of the glaring spotlight of isolation, or at least he was no longer alone there. To him she was an angel come to life. He felt her in his soul, as if she were his soul's companion. And yet as his body ached for her, this did not torment him. It filled him with vitality and joy. He breathed easily that night and looked forward to seeing her the next day.

The next morning, as he walked into the rehearsal hall, the cast could not conceal their elation at meeting their guest artist, the famous Salvatore DeCarlo. Some bombarded him with adulation, some flirted with him, while others kept an awed distance. He was very friendly, able to graciously accept all this attention while still being respectful to all, and genuinely interested in knowing everyone as an equal. He asked everyone to call him Salvo as his friends and family did. He made everyone feel like a friend.

"He's very strong," Theresa thought.

When the tumult of his entrance settled down, Max brought Salvo over to meet Theresa who had waited quietly by the rehearsal piano. The atmosphere of the room changed as they stood close together. They wordlessly nodded at one another.

Max, feeling the intensity of their chemistry, didn't want to waste a moment. He knew he had captured lightning in a bottle.

He said, "Let's have some fun. Let's begin with your duet: *Libiamo*." The rehearsal pianist began the introduction.

From the first instant the two of them burst into the personas of

Alfredo and Violetta like two flames combusting into an inferno, wildly in love, ignited by a passion so heated that it could only exist in the moment. One that they didn't know was within them. One that they hadn't known existed. They sang like they had never sung before, animated by a new incalculable power, intoxicated and delirious, as the song called for Violetta and Alfredo to be. They weren't ready yet to find out if it stopped there.

Rehearsals continued in this way for the next few weeks. Each fully aware that they carried an enormous professional burden, which demanded that they keep their passion focused into their performances. They were exhilarated knowing that they would not disappoint the considerable expectations that had been placed on them. Each one was careful not to do anything to break the spell. They kept their personal distance.

Max kept a watchful eye on Theresa. He understood what she was feeling. He had confidence in her professionalism and strength of character to be able to handle this. And she knew he was there if she needed him. He and the company were over the moon. This was going to be a production for the ages.

Outside of rehearsal Theresa and Salvo kept mostly to themselves. They enjoyed an occasional dinner at Escoffier's with Max, other cast members, and the soldiers, whom Max had invited when encountering them on the streets of Paris. These dinners were surreal to Theresa and Salvo. The food was superb. The wine was superb. Everything seemed lit up. They barely spoke to one another, but they were together. They were in a place beyond words.

The other women flirted outrageously with Salvo as they attempted to engage him in conversation about the book by Gaston Leroux; *The Phantom of the Opera.* They joked about the Phantom's presence at the Palais Garnier and the underground lake that actually existed, below the opera house. They warned him to beware the massive chandelier which had once crashed into the audience, as was documented in Leroux's book. Everyone was intrigued with these stories. But to Salvo these conversations were only noise in the background. Salvo was tuned only to Theresa and she to him. They were at the center of all things paradoxical. A place that cannot be found until it finds you. It had found them and they could not escape. They were prisoners, not of the Phantom, but of something beyond explanation, and beyond their control.

Later in their rooms they would tremble. They had never felt like this before. They had both performed many heroines and heroes who experienced passion and tragedy because of love. What they had experienced in those performances was transcendence. The composer's beautification of the human condition was theirs to interpret. Their job was to provide the audience with a unified and compassionate glimpse into humanity that would hopefully result in the knowing of their own hearts and souls. As artists Theresa and Salvo's detached spirits were free to allow these characters to animate them, speak through them and then leave them. It was a thrilling experience with no lasting consequences. But now their spirits were no longer detached but on fire. Not only were their characters on stage, but they themselves were also present, blazing, body, heart and soul.

Theresa and Salvo were growing anxious for the first week of April and opening night. They were ready. Everyone was ready. They were confident in their performances. They had learned at a distance, that their passion had a life of its own. It revealed itself to them, one incorruptible moment at a time. They were anxious to find out what would come next.

The excitement of the opening night crowd was unparalleled. Everyone in Paris who could get a ticket was there, from royalty and government officials to the everyday citizens and students who were true lovers of opera. Max had put tickets aside so that soldiers could attend. He had been doing this from the onset of the war. Afterwards they were always invited backstage to shake hands with the cast.

From the moment they stepped on stage Salvo and Theresa's voices filled the theatre with a manic ecstasy that left the audience drunk with sensation. It was an intoxicating cocktail of transcendent beauty and the erotic heat of unquenchable desire. Each of their voices was exquisite in its own beauty, but their combined voices were a force of nature. The elemental energies spoke through them with all the fury and harmony, destruction and regeneration of nature. They were the instruments of heaven, and the eternal song that sang them vibrated in the hearts and souls of the audience.

When Alfredo took Violetta in his arms and masterfully waltzed her around the ballroom in her breathtaking gown, the audience felt each dizzying twirl and nimble step as if the shoes on their feet had become their own. Each touch, by the lovers, sent warm sensual waves of energy through the audience member's bodies. The frenzy of each kiss left them gasping as their heart's raced. Violetta's death sent them plunging to the depths of despair, then elevated once again, by the beauty of Verdi's music, to an awareness of death and destiny.

The applause washed over them like tidal waves of electricity. The curtain call was a thunderous standing ovation, passionate, with tears, joy, shouting and the pounding of hands together, and feet on the floor. The curtain calls were countless.

"*La Traviata* was a ride on a shooting star," the critics proclaimed.

"Never has the desperate joy or depths of anguish of these lovers been more profoundly realized than through the lens of these dazzling performers."

"An unequivocal triumph!"

The enthusiasm for this production had all of Paris abuzz. People spoke of nothing else. Theresa and Salvo had fulfilled their responsibility to carry the show.

In the days that followed the entire company basked in the glow of being the toast of Paris. Their performances would be lauded and talked about for many years to come. Now, for the remaining weeks of the run they would have time to explore Paris and enjoy the adulation and contentment of their success.

9

The antique shop on the Left Bank had been in the back of Theresa's mind throughout rehearsals, and now that opening night was over she had the time to go look for it. She hoped that the old book that the shop mistress had told her about was still there. Max was in meetings all day, so Theresa set off on her own. She felt adventurous, so instead of calling for Max's automobile she took a hired carriage.

She got off at Notre Dame and walked to the Left Bank of the Seine River that flowed through Paris. It was now a Spring day in April and perfect weather for a long walk. As she wandered the streets she saw that they were filled with soldiers. Several had lost limbs and some wore patches to cover missing eyes and many had come from the hospital camp, in Etaples, where their surgeries had taken place. As she walked, she thought about her brother Robert, now an Ensign. He was on a navy ship escorting merchant ships through the Straits of Gibraltar, trying to keep them safe from German torpedoes. He was now married with a child. His wife, Gwendolyn, and his child Katherine were at home in Wisconsin being looked after by Greta and Annie while Robert served his country. Claude was traveling in Germany, where the opera company would be appearing next. He would be attending their opening night there. The happening at Timber Lake was no longer actively remembered, but still, when Theresa thought of her father it was with the respect due a parent, but void of emotion, and certainly not with love.

As Theresa passed the soldiers she smiled and nodded good day to them. She hoped that Robert, wherever he was, was being treated with kindness. She said a silent prayer for his safety and his return to their family. She prayed for all the soldiers so far from home, many of whom were lonely and suffering. She prayed for the end of the war.

She had carefully kept the card with the shop's address and now took it out of her handbag to study it. It was only steps away from where she stood.

The display window was crowded with old dishes, silver services, jewelry and ornamental objects. It was backed by a red velvet curtain, which blocked the sun from the interior of the shop. As she entered, she found that the small space was crowded and a little shabby. It was full of interesting, discarded pieces of furniture, shelves of books, lamps, piles of fabrics and all kinds of things, each one with a history and a story to tell. She stopped at what appeared to be the proprietor's desk and waited for him to appear. Up against the wall were some old stained-glass windows. The one she stood before was rose, gold, blue and green with a mandala of the Blessed Virgin at its center. It caught her attention, and for a moment she was transfixed.

"How beautiful," she thought to herself. "I wonder where it came from."

She was startled by a small, mustached, older Frenchman, as he entered from a back room. He smiled a warm smile.

"*Bonjour Monsieur,*" she greeted him. "The shop mistress from the Palais Garnier was here a few weeks ago and bought some antique fabric from you," she began.

"*Oui Mademoiselle,*" the proprietor exclaimed. "She had told me that it was for you Mademoiselle Berto, for Violetta in *La Traviata*."

He had recognized her. He was excited but dignified, displaying impeccable manners as he spoke to her in broken English.

"I have seen your opening night most thrilling," he continued, "And am most honored to meet you, *la chanteureuse*, most dazzling, *au-delà de toute description*." He reached for her hand and kissed it.

"I'm so delighted that you attended our opening," she replied, "And I am very happy that you were able to see the beautiful gown that was made for me from the fabric purchased from you. We were so lucky to have found it. I am most grateful to you."

He smiled warmly.

"I have come to see if you still have the basket containing the book of music that was with the fabric," she concluded.

"*Oh Oui Mademoiselle Berto! Oui!*" He could not contain his glee at being able to please her. "It has been looked at by a gentleman my wife has told me, *mais pas de vente*...how you say... 'no sale'. Please to allow me, I will fetch it for Mademoiselle from the dust of the shelves. You wait *un moment*."

He left to wind his way through the crowded shop. As she obediently waited, feeling jubilant that the book had not been sold, a figure appeared in the doorway blocking out the sunlight for an instant. He looked to be a dark figure silhouetted in a halo of golden sunlight. He cast a long shadow, which engulfed her. As he entered, the light flooded back in behind him. She saw that it was Salvatore DeCarlo.

Salvo saw at once that it was her. They stood looking at each other in disbelief that they actually existed outside of the theatre. Suddenly the shop was transformed into the most beautiful place on earth. The objects housed there seemed to come alive, each piece of furniture, each crystal goblet, each book, everything in the little shop responded to being seen by the loving eyes of Salvo and Theresa. In the warmth of their gaze they were reminded what it was like to be seen as beautiful and useful once more, and they glowed.

"Signorina Berto." He spoke her name as if it were a prayer. He reached for her hand to kiss it as they stood, framed by the stained glass window of the Virgin Mary.

As his hand enfolded hers she was transported. She felt that she was in a holy place. He raised her gloved hand to his lips and kissed it softly, humbly, while looking into her eyes.

"Your servant," he said softly.

As he raised his mouth from her silk covered hand he did not release it, which drew her closer to him. His eyes never left hers and as hers grew wide his grew narrow and penetrating. Every nerve in their bodies was awake and receptive. At this moment the proprietor was approaching with the basket.

"Mademoiselle, I have found it." He stopped, stunned, to see Salvatore standing there with Theresa.

"Oh Monsieur DeCarlo! *Mon Dieu*! This is *incroyable*...how you say...amazing! I have seen you and Mademoiselle in *La Traviata*. Monsieur is *l'artiste superbe*! I am so honored for you to be here with Mademoiselle Berto! *Mon Dieu! Mon Dieu!*"

Salvatore and Theresa smiled at the sweet man. Then seeing the book Salvo said, "*Monsieur*! This is the book I came back for. When I saw it before I did not have any French francs with me to buy it, so I told the proprietress, your wife, that I would come back!"

"I came here today looking for this book as well!" Theresa exclaimed in astonishment.

"*Mon Dieu!*" the proprietor uttered.

"Well then you must have it!" Salvo declared taking the book from the basket.

As he put it in her hands, they both felt the constraints of time fall away. They stood, each of them with their hands on the book, before the image of the Blessed Virgin, feeling as if they were floating in space, but at the same time they were aware of their feet kissing the earth, and the pulsing in their bodies.

Theresa spoke first. "You must have it. I want to give it to you as a gift."

The proprietor chimed in, "I will give it to both parties as a gift! You will take the basket with the book! It is my absolute most pleasure. I beg of you to please accept my gift to always remember this amazing day!"

They all laughed with pure joy.

"We must give you something as well," Theresa said to the dear man, "so that you too will remember us and our meeting." Then looking around she asked, "Do you have a piece of paper and a pencil. I will make you a drawing!"

"I beg you, *un moment s'il vous plait,*" the excited little man replied as he disappeared to fetch a paper and pencil.

Salvo and Theresa were still holding the book.

"I don't even know what is in the book," Theresa said softly, "I only heard about it from the shop mistress and it interested me."

"It is a very old book of sacred music. Music that was sung in the Catholic masses centuries ago," Salvo explained.

"The shop mistress told me that a German peasant found it in the Black Forest in the ruins of a convent," Theresa told him. "It was in a stone cupboard along with the fabric from which my ball gown was made. "

They stood in silence for a moment.

"Please," she continued, "I want so much for you to have the book. I feel that it was meant for you to have it, and for me to give it to you". She released her hands from the book.

It was impossible for him to contradict her. "I will treasure it always," Salvo said reverently.

The proprietor returned with some clean white paper and a sharp black pencil. Theresa took them and deftly sketched a portrait of the proprietor so lovely that it brought tears to his eyes. Both she and Salvo signed it for him. Then she opened the book of sacred music and on the cover page quickly sketched a portrait of Salvo. She signed it, not with her name, but with the words, "Love is eternal, and eternity is now."

"The Mademoiselle has given you a gift and now I want to give you one as well," Salvo began. "I hope I am not presumptuous in hoping that you and your wife would enjoy seeing *La Traviata* again."

The proprietor was dumb founded.

"I humbly ask you to be my guest, if you so choose, at our performance tomorrow evening. I will have the tickets brought to you by our driver," Salvo concluded.

"Oh that is most kind Monsieur, most kind. My wife she will not believe! *Mon Dieu*!"

They bid their dear new friend adieu and left the shabby little store where they had found such happiness. As they walked outside, the Left Bank was bright with the noonday sunshine, and fragrant with the scent of flowers from the stalls that dotted the streets. A gypsy boy played a romantic tune on a concertina with a tender passion, and the streets were filled with lovers.

"Shall we walk for a little while?" Salvo asked. "Shall we walk to Notre Dame Cathedral?"

"Oh yes," Theresa replied. "We must go to Notre Dame."

Salvo had come in Max's car. As he handed the driver the basket containing the book, he told him to meet them at Notre Dame later that day.

Salvo longed to take Theresa's hand but at the same time he wanted her to move freely so that he could take in her every move. As they walked along the *rive gauche*, as the Parisians called the Left Bank, he delighted in her graceful steps, the way her hair moved in the breeze, the turn of her head and the blush in her cheeks. Her stark shadow on the pavement and her shimmering reflection in the Seine River enchanted him. They moved slowly so that they could look at one another and talk. He told her that his name was really Michael Salvatore DeCarlo, but from a very young age everyone called him by his middle name, Salvatore, and then Salvo. They told each other things that they had never told anyone else. He told her about his years at the seminary and his study of sacred scripture and music. He told her of his agony that his brothers were fighting the war while he lived a life of luxury. She told him of her nightmare of the tortured little bird and how her brother showed her how to set it free, and of its return to her as a white bird bringing her salvation. By the time they reached Notre Dame they had shared the most intimate details of their lives. The one thing Theresa did not share with Salvo was what happened at Timber Lake.

Theresa led Salvo to a spot outside of Notre Dame where a wooden post stood.

"This post marks the absolute center of Paris," she began. "It is called Point Zero! All roads in Paris and in all of France begin and end at this very spot! This is where the guillotine once stood so that the priests could come from the cathedral to pray for those about to be executed," she continued.

Salvo moved very close to Theresa so that they both stood on the spot together.

"So many blessings and so much pain," Salvo said in a whisper. "Such is the way of this world."

As they stood close they were drawn together and, like two magnets, they were unable to resist what was ignited in each by the other. First their eyes met, then their hands joined, then their mouths tenderly touched uniting them to the sacred geometry of the spot. They were intrinsically joined to the matrix of meridians that began and ended at their kiss. The topography of the network lit up and surrounded them with vibrant colors and pulsing sensations, not visible, but present and known only to true lovers. Their mouths clung together as if never to be parted. And then they stood breathlessly enfolded tight in each other's arms.

It was the ringing of the cathedral bells that awakened them from this rapture, beckoning to them to enter. In the ringing of the bells they heard the voice of Notre Dame. It contained a loving presence that resonated in their hearts, and in those of all citizens and visitors. Their unifying sound was assurance that no one need ever be lonely in Paris: young, old, loved, unloved, worthy or unworthy. The bells spoke to all hearts as to an intimate companion, unconditionally, in joyful communion, without preference or judgment, as they now spoke to Theresa and Salvo.

Theresa and Salvo passed through the huge doors of the cathedral, which were adorned with ironwork so exquisite that it was once rumored that their creator, Biscornet, had sold his soul to the devil, for no human hand was capable of such intricate artistry. Inside, high up above the doors, the light shown through the rose-colored mandala into the nave, which stretched before them under the high, rib-vaulted ceiling. It was a holy place. Some said this was because of its placement over an energy vortex, and its enlightened construction designed to inspire reverence and awe. But aside from its masterpiece of construction, the atmosphere itself was holy by virtue of the humble and pure of heart, who for centuries gathered here to be healed of trauma, to renew their strength, to express their abiding faith, to pray for intercession, to dispel bitter disillusionment and to be whole again, at one with their creator. All of the cruel deeds done in the name of God and religion could not diminish the centuries of miracles that had been granted here. They filled the air like soft halos left echoing behind to sustain the souls of those in need.

After first dipping their fingers into the holy water font and blessing themselves, Theresa brought Salvo to the statue of St. Theresa. She often came here to pray when in Paris. They each lit a candle and then knelt side by side. As soon as they closed their eyes to pray, they felt the holy water expand into a veil covering them with a blissful warmth that dissolved all feelings of being alone. They entered into a meditative state where each breath connected them to a higher power. They found themselves to be kneeling under a beam of bright light from which flowed a power that could only be described as the source of all Divinity. Within it there was no separation. All was peace and understanding. From this source flowed the wisdom of the ages to be received as easily as breathing for those who sought it. Their prayerful hands reached out to each other, and as they touched this sustaining grace flowed through them as one body, one soul, one heart, and one mind, uniting them to one another and to the Divinity under which they knelt. Theirs was a sacred union.

Afterwards they lingered in the cathedral, not wanting this morning to ever end. They marveled at the holy relics housed there, and then just sat quietly in the pews relishing the majesty that surrounded them and the occurrences of this providential day. Their minds had been opened up to many new thoughts.

They thought about all the true believers who had come to this holy place over the centuries. The many people of all religions and races, who had come to experience what they had experienced: the timeless connection to the divine, free of religious dogma and belief systems. They thought of a passage from the Bible: "for in my father's house there are many mansions," and they thought about the many paths to divinity. They thought about the connection between time, conscious thought, and language. They marveled that they felt they were in a dream and yet fully awake in their bodies, experiencing the miracle of being alive, and being together.

After a while they had to once again acknowledge the outside world. They had to leave to meet Max's driver at the designated time. They had to return to the Ritz to prepare for that evening's performance.

10

The next two weeks were the happiest Theresa and Salvo had ever known. Their lives, spread out before them, were a corridor of open doors. They were the toast of Paris, their performances were on fire, and they were in love. With the show under control Theresa and Salvo allowed themselves to be wined, dined and celebrated without reservation. Max saw their joy and was genuinely happy for them. But he worried. Theresa was a singer. Would she give up her career to be a wife and mother? What would that do to her? Salvo was a devout Catholic. He had wanted to be a priest. Would he really be happy as the father of a big family? He would be there if either of them wanted his counsel, but for now he thought that they deserved this experience. They were young, in love, and on top of the world.

As Theresa and Salvo spent more time together, their bodies ached to be closer, to be united as one. Their embraces grew closer and deeper, and as their mouths hungered to be joined, their whole bodies now burned with desire to be joined. They longed to come together in every way that was closer and deeper. What was once a heavenly fire lit in an imaginary world was now a carnal reality in which that they burned. It was consuming them. They were more and more out of control in their time together. All they wanted was to be alone touching and kissing, clinging to each other in breathless longing. They were ecstatically happy.

One night, after a performance which had garnered many curtain calls, once she and Salvo had said a tender goodnight, Theresa lie in bed with Merlin purring at her feet. Instead of her usual deep, dreamless sleep she had a nightmare.

She was a little pony. She was not a wild pony but was bridled, with a bit in her mouth, so that she could be led about performing tricks for an adoring crowd. She loved being petted, adored and cared for. She loved the cheering of the crowd as she did her tricks. She didn't wish to be free of her trainers. She loved them. She was content. All at once a man's hand took her by the neck to gain control of her. He tried to take the bit out of her mouth. She bucked and kicked and cried out but he would not let go. She did not want him to set her free. She didn't want to roam in the wilderness, to face the cold of the winter, to starve and to feel the indifference and cruelty of strangers. She didn't know this man. His face was hidden from her.

Then the dream changed.

She was barefoot, dirty and dressed in rags. Her hands were bound, and she was on a wooden cart with many other women of her age. She was being taken to the guillotine to be beheaded. She did not know what crime she had committed for which she was to be put to death. She was screaming in terror for help, but the crowds only laughed and jeered at her as the cart rolled down the cobblestone streets to the waiting guillotine standing before Notre Dame Cathedral. The procession of priests came out to give a final blessing to the doomed women. As they prayed Theresa realized that she was standing at Point Zero. She knew she must die, for her life began and ended at this point.

She woke up in a cold sweat. Merlin was sitting on her chest looking into her eyes in alarm. She sat up in bed holding Merlin as thoughts flooded her mind. What if she got married? She had never wanted a family beyond the one she already had. She had never wanted to do anything else but sing. Who would she be if she wasn't a singer? She had no real identity outside of her artistry. Would Salvo come to despise her as she lost all that was special about her? Would she come to despise him for continuing with his career while she raised his children? She thought about her mother and for the first time acknowledged thoughts that she had dared not consider before. Had Greta squandered her youth, beauty, humor, and gift for unconditional love, on a man who abused her? A man who didn't know how precious she was? A man who turned her into someone invisible because of the uncertainty that he surrounded her with? And yet, her mother loved her father with all her heart. She then remembered how she and her mother watched a butterfly break out of its cocoon. Her mother explained to her that a caterpillar had to create a cocoon where it digested itself in order to turn into a butterfly. She shuddered to think of it. Is this what women do? Digest themselves to turn into wives and mothers? Are they really reconfigured into something more beautiful? Yet she and Salvo had been given something so special. Something that all people are seeking and many never find. She could never deny her sacred bond with him. Was it her destiny to be his wife and mother to his children? Did she want to devote her life to being be a lover, a wife and a mother? How could she know the identity of her soul? Her relationship with Salvo had always revealed itself one moment at a time. It was beyond her control. She couldn't predict, what had thus far existed only in the present moment. She would not yield to confusion. She would have faith in all the miraculous things that had happened between them. Merlin's gentle purring comforted her and as she lay back down, she fell asleep.

They had two more weeks in Paris. Then they had a week's lay off before they opened in Germany in May. The performances were better than ever, the theatre was packed, and all were happy, but then, some of the company members fell ill with what they were told was the flu. There had been whispers among the soldiers that this was a flu that the government was keeping secret because of the war. It was called the Spanish Flu. Many of the soldiers were sick with it. It was whispered that it was being spread by the soldiers on military ships that traveled from port to port.

The show went on even though they were missing a few company members, but then the unimaginable happened. One of them died. And then more became sick. Max called the company together for a meeting to discuss this tragedy. Theresa noticed that Max didn't look as he usually did. He looked tired and pale. Max stood before them speaking words of comfort and reassurance when he suddenly collapsed. They all cried out in fear and jumped to their feet, surrounding him.

"Call a doctor!" Theresa commanded, and someone immediately complied. Salvo and the other men carried Max to his room.

After examining him the Doctor reported back to the anxious cast members that Max had the flu. Although it was claiming many victims, it was not yet thought to be any more dangerous than other flus. With Max's consent the doctor hired a private nurse to care for him. The doctor would visit him daily. All hoped for the best.

The thought of losing Max was more than Theresa, or any of the others could bear. But because of the company's respect for him and the professional standard that was his hallmark, they continued to perform their very best, as he would have demanded. When not on stage, Theresa and Salvo were at his bedside doing whatever the nurse allowed them to do for him.

Over the next week other members fell ill. From his sick bed Max saw to it that they also received the same care that he was receiving. Max's condition worsened. His fevers were high and his breathing labored. Now, he was unconscious most of the time. All prayed for his recovery and the realization that he was not getting better made their hearts heavy. Still they hoped for the best. No one seemed to know too much about this flu. But the French government did know. It was infecting the entire world. But it was being kept quiet because of the war.

After the many ovations of closing night there was no party. Instead all rushed to Max's room to share with him their triumph. They were hoping to find him feeling better but instead found his condition had worsened. Seeing how sick he was they called for the Doctor. When he arrived he was besieged with requests that Max be taken to the hospital. The Doctor told them that at the hospital he would only be put in a ward with others sick with the flu. He reassured them that here he had his own room and more immediate and personal attention. He could not tell them whether Max would make it through the night and survive or if he would die. It could go either way. They were now hoping to have one last moment with the man they all loved so dearly. They stayed there till early morning, each of them whispering their loving messages in his ear. As the dawn breeze sent a chill through the room, he opened his eyes and spoke softly to Theresa who kept vigil at his side, his hand in hers.

"Whatever happens, don't despair," he whispered. "With despair comes a forgetfulness. You mustn't forget who you are," he continued. "Be strong." He looked into her eyes and smiled a beautiful smile. "You are the best friend I have ever had. I love you." Theresa's tears fell upon his hand.

Then looking up at the company members he rallied his strength. Because he could barely whisper, they were all still and silent as they hung onto his every word.

"I love you all. It has been my privilege to know you. I am very grateful. 'My cup runneth over'."

He closed his eyes and left his body as he had lived his life, with kindness and dignity.

Theresa sobbed as she clutched his lifeless hand. Salvo reached for her and she turned to sob in his arms.

The people of Paris were becoming sick with the Spanish Flu. But they were being told that it was under control and not to panic. The soldiers whispered of quarantines, but none were imposed. Life went on as usual although there was a feeling of fear that hung over the city. At first the company waited to hear if their tour would be canceled, but Max was so organized that even after his death his assistant could step in and take over seamlessly. Opera houses in Europe would remain open. Over the next few days the company was preparing to go to Germany after their lay over in Paris.

On their final day at the Ritz, Salvo and Theresa planned one last breakfast to remember Max and all the good things that had happened before the flu changed their lives forever. Theresa was late. This wasn't like her. She was always considerate of others and was not one to keep anyone waiting. As Salvo waited for Theresa a feeling of dread came over him. With the sound of every person who entered the restaurant he would sit up straight, breathing a sigh of relief, sure it was her—but it wasn't. Suddenly a panicked realization came over him. He jumped up from his seat and ran up the many flights of stairs and down the endless corridors to her room. Before he got to her door he heard Merlin yowling in distress. Salvo immediately pounded on the door. He called out her name. Tears poured down his face as he pounded on her door and called to her. A chambermaid heard him and hurried over to assist him.

"Please," Salvo exclaimed, "I need the key!" he cried. "Please help me! I need to open her door!"

The little woman fumbled through her keys and found the one to fit the lock. Salvo pushed the door open. Theresa lay there covered in sweat and gasping for air.

"Get the doctor," Salvo told the chambermaid. "Please hurry!"

Salvo had never felt so helpless. He took her in his arms and held her body against his. She was burning up with fever.

"Theresa my darling," he began, knowing that he must be strong, "I'm here now. Everything will be all right. The doctor is on the way."

"Salvo," she whispered, "I'm sorry darling." He held her close, rocking her in his arms.

The doctor confirmed the worst. Theresa had the Spanish Flu. Salvo notified the new company manager of her illness and that he would be staying behind to care for her. Their understudies would have to take over their roles. The entire company was in a state of shock. He telegraphed her father in Germany and her mother in Wisconsin. Her brother was at sea and could not be reached.

He consulted with the doctor as to what would be the best plan for Theresa's recovery. They decided that she be cared for privately rather than in a hospital.

Their rooms at the Ritz were no longer available after that night, and it would be better for her to be in a place where there were not travelers from all over the world coming and going. So Salvo found a quiet flat near the *Arc de Triomphe* where the doctor could tend to her on a daily basis. A private nurse was hired. Once there, Salvo devoted himself to her care. When the nurse would allow, he fed her hot broth, vegetable juice, and ginger tea. He heated pots of water and helped her to inhale the steam as he sat her up in bed. He put cold compresses on her forehead to break her fever. Some days were better than others. His life was like a swinging pendulum going from joy to terror by the day, sometimes by the hour. Some days she was strong enough to talk in a whisper.

"We are so lucky," she whispered. "When I met you it was like going into a room that I never knew existed. Everything was so new and yet I felt that I had always known you, had always been with you. It was the world that was new. I was seeing it for the first time instead of turning away, because you were there. And you made everything that I feared beautiful. I was new too. You were the longing in my heart, the faith in my soul. I loved you before I met you, and now I realize that I had always been searching for you. Asking God for you. And I was lucky enough to find you and to see myself as you saw me."

"We're going to be married, Theresa," he would tell her. "We will have a home with children and our home will be so full of love that our lives will be heaven on earth because you will be there. "

"We are married," she whispered. "We were married by God in Notre Dame Cathedral. "

Within days her distraught father was at their door. He brought with him a renowned doctor from Germany. They consulted with the French doctor to be sure that all the most current treatments were available to Theresa. Everything was being done for her: aspirin, epinephrine, oxygen injected under the skin, salt of quinine, even cinnamon powder in milk. The German doctor proposed something brand new: Digitalis administered intravenously. It was not in widespread use but was the highest biomedical technological treatment available. They all agreed that this must be tried.

Once Claude was sure that everything possible was being done for her, he allowed himself to sit by her bedside. His anguish was immeasurable. His beautiful daughter whom he had done such irreparable harm to might be dying. He wanted to express all his regret, all his remorse, all his love, but felt consummately unworthy. He sat, as if paralyzed, with tears streaming down his face. If only he could turn back time. If only they could start all over. If only he could be given another chance. He had kept distant from her all these years accepting her coldness, knowing that it was what he deserved. He couldn't ask for her forgiveness because he didn't feel worthy of it. So he sat quietly, inside the whirlwind that was his sickness, and prayed. Somehow Theresa heard his prayers and opened her eyes to look at him. She saw a man crying, praying and suffering. He was her father. He was not the father she had protected herself from by withholding her love, but a man she wanted to comfort, heal and give her love to.

"Father," she whispered, "Please don't cry."

He was stunned to hear her speak. "Theresa," he said through his tears, unsure of himself in her presence.

"Take my hand Father," she continued.

He had not touched her in so long that he was like a starving man as he gratefully took her hand.

"I am sorry to have made you so unhappy," she whispered.

"No!" he cried out. "You have never made me unhappy. You have never made anyone unhappy. I am the one. I am the one who is guilty. Please forgive me Theresa. Please forgive me. "

"I forgive you Father," she replied. "You must forgive yourself."

"I can't," he cried as he buried his head in her hand in abject shame. "I can never forgive myself for the evil I have done," he sobbed.

"Will you do something for me Father?" she whispered, her voice growing even weaker. "Go the Notre Dame Cathedral and kneel before the shrine of St. Theresa. Ask her to intercede with God for your forgiveness."

Theresa was drifting off into unconsciousness again. The nurse asked Claude to let her rest now.

Claude walked the streets of Paris, crazed, sick with self-loathing. Theresa had asked him to forgive her. What had he done to his innocent child? Again he considered suicide. Then he heard the bells of Notre Dame ringing. They penetrated the malevolence of his sickness and he felt them in his very soul. He remembered what Theresa had asked of him. He made his way to Notre Dame and knelt at the shrine of St. Theresa. As he knelt, he felt the whirlwind around him calm and dissipate. As he breathed, he felt Theresa in every breath. She was restoring him in this holy place. He prayed for Theresa's recovery. He asked God to take him in her place. And then he heard her soft voice repeating:

"Ask her to intercede with God for your forgiveness."

He felt a shift in his being. He felt that his soul was stronger than his body, stronger than his sickness. His soul became illuminated by a bright light, under which he knelt. He was joined to a higher power that was all forgiving, all understanding, all loving and all mighty. To be united to this power was to be restored and cleansed, because here there was no sin. His forgiveness of himself was only to live in this light.

These words came alive within him:

"He restoreth my soul. He leadeth me in the paths of righteousness for his name's sake. Yea though I walk through the valley of the shadow of death, I will fear no evil: for thou art with me."

This was a living and immediate experience, no longer words on paper. No begging and pleading with an angry judgmental God, no self-hatred and supplication, but unification with this benevolent source of healing and restoration. He understood for the first time what it meant to worship. He knelt, united to this power, for a long time. He now knew how to pray. He now knew how to forgive. He was given the second chance he was seeking.

He visited Theresa every day. He sat at her bedside holding her hand while pouring out his love to her. Everything he had never told her he now shared with her. He told her about how he would listen to her practice on the piano he had given her and how happy that made him. He told her about every performance she had given, his favorite moments and how filled with pride and love he had felt to know that she was his daughter. She sometimes responded by squeezing his hand or smiling slightly in her sleep like state. He stayed as long as he was allowed to, and then walked the streets of Paris, often returning to Notre Dame to pray, or just to sit in its holy atmosphere.

Although he didn't know what had caused such estrangement between Theresa and her father, Salvo was deeply moved to have witnessed what was occurring between them now, and the peace it was bringing to both of them.

Salvo loved Theresa with all his heart. He would hold her. He would kiss her. He had no fear of getting sick. He wanted to go wherever she was going. But he didn't get sick. And she didn't get better. It was two weeks after she was initially stricken that things changed. Before, when he held her close, he could feel the battle for survival going on inside her. Now she felt far away as if she was attached to her body by only a thin thread. When he closed his eyes he could see her far away, sleeping on wind.

11

At the same time, about a thousand miles away from Paris, Robert's naval ship was on assignment in the Atlantic Ocean escorting a merchant ship through the Strait of Gibraltar. The Strait lies between Africa and Europe and connected the Atlantic Ocean to the Mediterranean Sea. There were strong currents flowing through it: eastward from the Atlantic and westward from the Mediterranean. Their plan was to be carried through the Strait by the eastward currents under the cloak of dark night in order to evade detection by enemy German submarines. Robert was on the deck studying the constellations of Scorpio and Sagittarius. He was thinking about how countless ancient mariners had studied this same night sky, when an enemy submarine successfully fired on his ship with multiple torpedoes.

As the deck exploded and splintered, Robert was thrown through the air into the ocean. He plunged beneath the surface into the pitch black of its depths. He fought his way to the surface and treaded water as he was carried farther away from the wreckage by a strong current. The water was surprisingly warm, but still Robert knew that he was injured because he could feel the warmth of his blood in contrast to the water. He had a searing pain in his right shoulder and in his legs, and his arm was useless to him. Still he struggled to keep treading water with one arm.

The current carried him farther and farther away from the wreckage into the dark moonless night, lit only by the stars. Hours passed when, too tired to go on, he tried to rest by floating in the turbulent sea. He was so weak that he began to accept death as inevitable. As he struggled to remain conscious he heard the piercing cry of a bird. Too weak to look for it he continued floating the best he could. Then he heard it again, and then again. There was an urgency in the bird's call that roused him. He shifted his position to look for it. And then he saw its outline in the starlight. It seemed to be floating on the water. It shrieked again. It was calling out directly to him. His exhausted mind suddenly became alert.

"It must be sitting on something," he thought. "Something that is floating."

He struggled to swim in the direction of its cries. Within minutes he came upon a bird sitting on some planking blown from the deck of his doomed ship. It took all of his strength to climb up onto it. It was like a small raft. He lay there panting, delirious with gratitude. Then he searched the dark water for sight of any of his shipmates. He called out. But he saw no one nor received a response to his calls. The bird didn't fly away. It sat calmly, quietly, watching him until he finally collapsed, succumbing to his exhaustion.

As he slept he dreamed that his sister was there with him. He was reading to her, as he used to, from his book about King Arthur.

"He wore a large sword at his side and smelled like the movement of water and wind."

"Courage must be firmer, heart the bolder, spirit must be the greater as our strength grows less," he read to her.

It was beautiful to be with his sister again, and to once more be inspired by the words of Arthur.

"Oh dire, dreadful death you drag your heels. Why dawdle and draw back. You drown my heart."

He slept in this reverie until the bird awakened him with a shriek. It was warning him. He had moved too close to the edge of the raft. He mustn't slip into the dark water. He fell back asleep, under the watchful eye of the bird, which guarded him, until he was awakened by the first rays of the sun. In the light of day he could now see that his companion was a large white bird: a gull. As the sun rose higher over the horizon, they drifted for hours, carried by the current. He intently searched and listened for any sight or sound of other survivors. The gull sat beside him, calm and still. And then, as if summoned by an unheard command, the white bird shrieked and flew away. Robert felt a deep sadness at its departure. He knew it had saved him. He wished he could fly away too. He felt the helpless loneliness of confinement within his own body as the gull disappeared from sight. Robert was lost.

A group of fishermen had departed from the shores of Sardinia five days ago. They had fished the Mediterranean Sea and were now nearing British-controlled Gibraltar to deliver their catch. It was the final leg of their journey, and their work was completed. All had gone well. They were on deck enjoying the sunshine and calm waters when a white gull flew overhead, calling out to them. At first they paid little attention to it, but its persistent, piercing cries finally got their attention. It landed on the rail near an older fisherman named Paolo. He wore a patch over his eye and his hands were gnarled. As he turned to look at the bird, for a flickering of a second he thought he saw a woman: a lovely young woman with long dark hair.

"My mind must be playing tricks on me," he said to the other seamen as he looked at the gull. "For a second I thought I saw a woman!" Then the bird cried out again as if trying to communicate with him.

"This gull is talking to me," he declared. The other fishermen gathered close to the white bird as it sat, waiting for them, on the boat's rail.

The fishermen were from Sardinia, an island populated by generations of seamen, many of whom believed themselves to be the descendants of the lost city of Atlantis. They were a mystic people. The ancient philosopher Plato described them as "coming from the sea," and to this day the natives acknowledged their loyalty to Poseidon, the ruler of the ocean. The older men on board had spent many years on the water where they had often experienced unexplained events and mystic visions.

The gull again cried out directly to them, and then flew into the sky. In the swift flickering movement of its wings the other fishermen also saw the young woman.

"I see her too," was repeated amongst them. "She's telling us something!" One raised his binoculars to follow the gull's flight.

"There's someone out there," he said with certainty.

The men were aware of the enemy German submarines sent to demolish ships entering the Straits of Gibraltar. The possibility that survivors of these attacks might be out there was not far-fetched. They knew they would be safe sailing as far as Tangiers. Without hesitation they would follow the gull as far as they could.

As they neared Tarifa the gull again landed on their boat's rail. The men silently raised their binoculars and searched the surrounding waters. Having gained the seamen's rapt attention, the gull ascended into the sky again, beckoning them to follow. It flew to the raft, where Robert lay weak and in pain. It circled overhead calling out insistently, until Robert gathered his strength to sit up. Life flooded back into his wracked body at the sight of the gull. He saw the fishermen's boat in the distance. Painfully he rose to his feet. He began to frantically wave with his uninjured arm as he called out to them.

Paolo caught sight of him and exclaimed, "I see him! There's a sailor out there!"

The gull flew back and forth between the raft and the boat until the boat was close enough to lower a rope ladder. Robert, bleeding and in pain, swam to the boat. The fishermen helped him up the ladder and onto the safety of the deck. The gull landed on the rail close to Robert. Their eyes met and lingered lovingly for a few seconds. Then the gull silently flew away. Robert's eyes filled with tears as he watched it disappear over the sea. It was not seen again.

"Are there any others?" one of the seamen asked.

"I didn't see any, but there could be," Robert replied. "I was blown right into the eastward current, and it brought me into the Strait. There may be others that got caught in the westward current and are out in the Atlantic.

The Sardinians were heroic men and ready to help. But they were at a disadvantage. They knew they could not reach any other survivors in a reasonable amount of time in a boat powered by sails. They also knew that the British Navy would know of the attack by now and would be sending patrol vessels out to search for survivors. So they decided the best plan was to go to Gibraltar where Robert could report to the British Navy and be of assistance to them.

Robert's arm and shoulder were badly injured, so the men fashioned a makeshift sling for him and tended to his cuts and lacerations. Paolo, the man with the eye patch, held in his gnarled hands a canteen of water and some bread, which he offered to Robert who drank and ate hungrily.

As Robert drank and ate his fill he was reminded of the Arthurian poem: *The Lady of the Lake,* by Sir Walter Scott.

"The stag at eve had drunk his fill
Where danced the moon on Monan's rill...
Then, as the headmost foes appeared,
With one brave bound the corpse he cleared."

A voice interrupted his musings. It was Paolo, eager to tell him about the white bird. The others gathered around as Paolo told Robert that within the gull, he had been the first to see the soul of a beautiful young woman with long dark hair. Soon after, the others saw her too. The woman cried out to them and wouldn't give up until they followed her. She led them to Robert's raft, and to his rescue.

Robert was shaken to his core. He knew that the woman they described had been his sister. But it defied logic. How could she have even known that he was in danger? Could it really be possible that their love for one another had the power to open up a higher realm, where a miracle was granted them? Was it her soul that had inhabited the white gull? Was it her voice that had cried out to him? He studied the faces of the Sardinian fishermen. He was profoundly affected by their faith. They did not question the miraculous event that had just occurred, but instead willingly played a part in it. They didn't doubt it was real, but accepted it as a part of life, as real as any other part of life. Their fellowship with him caused a shift in his perceptions. During his years as a sailor he had spent a lot of time gazing at the sea and stars, longing to know the mysterious source that powered them. Now as he gazed over the sea, a veil lifted, and he experienced the mingling of the natural with the supernatural. Quickly and effortlessly he was being tuned to the sea, which acted as an undulating cosmic conductor, receiving and amplifying all the mysteries of the universe. The mysterious power that had eluded him now flowed through his body. What had only been a stirring in his soul was now integrated into his whole being. He was part of it. He was at one with it.

He felt a deep spiritual connection to the Sardinians, who by their stewardship, had brought him into the mystical realms imparted to seamen by the sea. He now knew why he had become a sailor instead of a soldier. He, like them, was born of the sea. He had found his destiny in the unification of his body and soul as a mystic seaman. The longing in his soul was satisfied. He was complete.

Led by Robert, and with the help of the fishermen's knowledge of the currents, the British Navy dispatched a second rescue party of patrol vessels. The first dispatch had rescued twelve men. The second dispatch was able to rescue many more. Some were found where Robert and the Sardinians led them, near Tangiers. Others were found outside the straits, in the Atlantic Ocean. They would never know the whole story of their rescue. Only Robert and the Sardinians knew.

After some time in the hospital Robert was being readied to be sent back to the United States. His shoulder had been fractured and his arm broken. His sharp shooting days were over. His original motivation to become an expert marksman had been forgotten long ago. This was a new chapter in his life.

Still bandaged, and with his arm in a sling, he said goodbye to the fishermen. A deep unspoken bond had formed between them. Robert would never know that his bond to Paolo was also a blood bond, or that their meeting was destined. Paolo would never know that he had saved the life of his grandson, or that the soul of the young woman he had seen was that of his dying granddaughter. There were few words at their parting. Just the unspoken love of fellow seamen, and the silent knowing of the supernatural events that had brought them together.

In their Paris flat Theresa was resting in Salvo's arms when she awoke with a sharp cry. Salvo soothed her, kissing her forehead and rocking her gently.

"Salvo," she whispered, "I was flying over the sea. Flying back to your arms. I had to tell you...you must know...I was afraid to love you. But now I know that it is an act of faith to love. And I have faith in you. Have faith in me."

Salvo tried not to weep. "I have faith in you my dearest love," he said softly, close to her ear. "I have faith in our love."

"Our love is eternal," she continued. "It is always present, like the light we knelt under in Notre Dame."

"Yes darling," Salvo answered kissing her face tenderly as she gently squeezed his hand.

"Wherever you go, no room will ever be empty. You are never alone."

"I am never alone. You are with me always Theresa." He kissed her warm lips as she drifted off into unconsciousness.

She uttered one more phrase so quietly she could barely be heard.

"Death itself is victory and a healing unto the soul." It was from the *Tales of Arthur*, but Salvo didn't know that.

"Don't speak of death my darling. You are going to live. We are going to be married and live together with our children for many happy years."

As Salvo spoke these words he knew that they were not true. He felt her hand weakly grasp his and then go limp. He kissed her and her lips were still warm. But he knew that the last words had been spoken. The last touch returned and the last pencil thin strand connecting her to life had been broken. She was gone.

At this moment his heart shattered, turned into dust and blew away. All the doors that had been opened to them were forever shut tight. He would never again be the man he was only a few moments ago.

Merlin climbed onto Theresa's chest and pushed his face against her mouth wanting to feel her breathe. Then he nestled by her side purring loudly and kneading her still warm, lifeless body, hoping it would come back to life. He looked up at Salvo and squinted his eyes tightly and then opened them wide in recognition of the sorrow they shared. Then he protectively laid across her body and cried.

Salvo woke the nurse. But there was nothing more to be done. The doctor was notified and was quickly on his way. Theresa's father arrived within the hour and quietly sat with Salvo by her bed wanting to be with her as long as possible. Then, once the doctor arrived they quietly made plans for her to be taken home to the United States to be buried in their family plot. Claude would take Merlin with him. He felt sure his granddaughter Katherine would love the cat and take good care of him. The cat clung to Salvo as Theresa's body was prepared to be moved.

The new company manager was called and told of her death. Arrangements were made for all money in her account to be transferred to her father's account. In the last few moments before Theresa's body was taken away, Salvo saw on the table next to her bed the book of music that had been the catalyst for their meeting in the antique shop. He knew he couldn't keep it. Even the sight of it threatened to unleash an avalanche of grief that would crush him.

"I know Theresa would want her family to have this," he told her father handing him the book. "Please," he continued, sensing her father's hesitation, "I want you to take it with you."

Her father touched the book reverently, knowing how much it must have meant to Theresa...to both of them.

"I'll treasure it," he began, "and I know this will mean a lot to her mother. Thank you."

Theresa's body was carried out of the door. Merlin left in the arms of Claude's chauffeur. Only Salvo and Claude remained in the room. They shared a final glance. Claude began to leave but stopped and turned back.

"I wish things could have been different," he said, his voice shaking with grief.

"I wish Theresa could have married you and had a family. I know you would have made her very happy. I wish you could have been a son to me. I wish you could have given me grandchildren." All Salvo could do was nod.

12

It was just after dawn. Theresa's body was gone. Everyone was gone. Salvo sat in a chair with his back to the window, alone and unable to move. He felt like an explosion had gone off inside his body leaving nothing but ashes in its wake. He couldn't cry. The pain left him numb, empty and stupefied. He could only feel the persistent ache of suffering, for not to be with Theresa was to suffer.

He could never again take his place among the happy people of the world. Among them he would be despised, as they guarded their happiness from those who suffered, with smug exclusivity. His memory was wiped clean of music, of God, of his family, of everything that had once defined him. Theresa had told him, "No room will ever be empty" but he couldn't remember. He couldn't remember anything. He could not endure the pain of remembering. He was alone in the dark. The only way out was to put one foot in front of the other, through a passage where the only light that shone was contained in the grace that mercifully appeared with each uncertain step.

Salvo sat for a long time, not eating or sleeping. Days passed with no awareness of them. A passage from the Bible kept repeating in his mind:

"They did not love their lives so much as to shrink from death."

It described the archangel Michael and his army. When at last Salvo got back out of his chair he was a different man. He would find kindred spirits only among those prepared to sacrifice themselves so that others may live. He would take his place alongside his brothers, on the battlefield of World War I.

The next few days were surreal. Salvo contacted the company manager to inform him that he would not be returning. He had decided to volunteer as infantry in the army. He wanted all money in his account to be sent to his family in Italy. The manager pleaded with him not to throw away his career and to return to the company. But that reality no longer existed for Salvo. Only the battle against omnipresent death was real to him now. The battlefield was where he wanted to be.

It was now June, and the German offensive on the Western Front was being fought. The troops were suffering massive casualties and the phrase "Backs to the Wall" headlined the newspapers and was on the lips of all patriotic citizens of Paris. The voluntary enlistments in France were smaller than those of Britain so the recruitment office eagerly accepted anyone who was willing to enlist without scrutiny.

After a brief period of training Salvo was sent into battle along with other volunteers and those conscripted citizen soldiers fulfilling their duty to bear arms in defense of their nation. It was a mass mobilization effort deploying much of the manpower of France as a "Nation in Arms". Most of them were sent as infantry to the Western Front to battle in the end days of the German offensive. Those surviving then fought at the Battle of the Amiens. Then in September of 1918 they were sent to fight in the Battle of Megiddo.

The men who fought at each other's sides throughout these battles came to love one another on a level that only exists on the battlefield. No one else could ever know what they had seen, what they had done, or the horrors they had endured. They persevered knowing that any minute might be the last for them or their combat brothers. They were committed to protecting their nation against those who would tear down the sanctity of their way of life, and to sacrificing themselves to protect one another.

The Battle of Megiddo was a British offensive led by Sir Edmund Allenby in the Sinai and Palestine Campaign, against the Ottoman Turks and their German allies. It was being fought in the valley of Megiddo also known to the Hebrews as the plains of Armageddon. The strategy was to encircle the enemy and cut off their escape routes. To achieve this, Allenby would use the infantry, cavalry, armored vehicles and aircraft.

Salvo and his unit were hunkered down in the trenches. For several days they had withstood shelling by the opposition. The sun was high in the sky and the thought, "it must be noon," had just passed through Salvo's mind, when a direct hit into their trench was made by the Turks. The sounds of men screaming in agony could be heard amidst the deafening sounds of explosions and gunfire in a hell-like cacophony. As bodies shattered, blood spurted into the air turning the gray smoke into red rain. Some of the soldiers lie dying, calling out for their mothers. Others were gone in an instant.

When the smoke cleared, the survivors saw that the trench was filled with the dead bodies of their brothers, some of them blown to pieces. On seeing this, one very young recruit snapped and lost his mind. He stood up screaming as he tore off his gas mask letting it fall into the muck of dead bodies, body parts, bone fragments and blood that he stood in. Salvo dove for the young boy and pulled him out of the line of fire. He tore off his own mask and put it over the boy's face. He held the young boy, trying to comfort him, atop the carnage that minutes ago was their comrades. He covered him as more shells barraged the trench and the shrapnel seared through their bodies.

Salvo thought, "This truly must be Armageddon. This must be the end of days."

The air was toxic with the smell of mustard gas. Some of the shells were loaded with this insidious substance that once inhaled or exposed to, could blind, incapacitate and even kill its target. Salvo had inhaled this gas willingly to save the boy. The medics came quickly, and along with the other survivors, they were transported to a medical camp.

The mustard gas took anywhere from three to twelve hours to take effect. So Salvo waited for the inevitable. After a while he felt searing pain in his throat and lungs. His skin became red and covered with blisters. The pain was so acute that he lost consciousness. The boy Salvo had rescued was treated for injuries caused by shrapnel, and for a broken leg. He had suffered minimal exposure to the mustard gas, but his leg had been shattered. He would walk with a crutch for the rest of his life. But now he sat vigil at Salvo's bedside. He wanted to care for his comrade who had sacrificed himself on the battlefield for his sake. As he sat he memorized every nuance of light and shadow that gave form to the objects and people, which inhabited the living world around him. He studied the shapes and planes of every face he saw, for if Salvo didn't regain his sight, the boy was preparing himself to be his eyes.

Salvo was given morphine for the pain. This kept him sedated. When he awakened, for only seconds at a time, he couldn't see anything. He could hear the doctors telling him that this blindness might be temporary, before he drifted back into his morphine-induced sleep. In this twilight sleep he heard music. Music, that had brought him unbearable sorrow in his waking state, now brought him soothing comfort and joy once more. He heard a choir of women singing *Salve Regina*. He could hear Theresa's voice among them. But she was far away. He couldn't take her in his arms as he had done only months ago, before his world was destroyed. But still, she was with him in his heart and soul. He was not alone. She would never be his wife, but she would be with him always. He had no knowledge of how long he laid in this dream like state, but he hoped it would never end. He was with Theresa. She sang for him. She talked to him. She brought him to the light that they had knelt under in Notre Dame Cathedral, and they rested there together.

When he awakened he could hear the young boy, sometimes weeping, sometimes praying. When he stirred, the boy told him the battle had been won. Then he would drift back into his twilight sleep.

Weeks passed, and then one day or night, for there was no difference to Salvo, he had a vision of Theresa that he had never had before.

He saw her before him, at his third eye point. She stood around two inches tall, and she was naked. Her nakedness was obscured because she was spinning. She spun, with her arms straight out to the side, as quickly as a spinning top. She spun from his right eye to his left eye, back and forth over and over again, gathering up in her spinning motion all that was foul and poisonous...all that brought darkness, damage and impairment...all that were the artifacts of chaos and destruction. Back and forth she spun until she had gathered up all the vile, corrupt, malevolent energy that had been inflicted upon Salvo. And then, with a swift upward movement of her arms she dispelled this dark energy into nothingness. In its place she released soft shimmering light, which flowed like water from her palms, now facing downwards, as she continued her spinning motion, bathing Salvo's eyes in a healing balm of grace. Then she stopped and stood at his third eye point. Her perfect stillness acted as a magnetic force drawing all the pieces of Salvo's broken body, mind and spirit together again. Focus replaced confusion as all unholy forces left him. His breathing became strong and steady once more. Life stirred within his body. Then, in a streak of light, she flew straight into the air and vanished, leaving Salvo to sleep.

When Salvo opened his eyes he found that he could see again. The room was very bright. He saw the boy sleeping in a chair next to his bed. He saw other beds with other soldiers, some of them from his unit. They filled the sun-drenched room. He tried to speak but barely a whisper came from his mouth.

"Where am I?" he whispered. No one heard him. He tried to speak louder.

"Where am I?" Again he could only utter a hoarse whisper.

His throat hurt when he spoke as did his lungs when he breathed. He reached over and touched the young boy who, startled by his touch, lunged forward.

"Where am I?" Salvo whispered again.

"You're in the hospital," the boy said eagerly, grateful that Salvo was awake. He spoke in a thick French accent. "You have been very sick for weeks," he continued.

"My name is Daniel Petelle. You saved my life." The boy began to weep.

"We are both alive," Salvo whispered. "Be happy."

The boy told Salvo how he had sat there day after day, week after week, praying for his recovery. He told him how ashamed he was of his cowardice that had caused Salvo to be injured and so desperately sick. He told him of his home in the French countryside and of his young wife, who was expecting their first child.

"If it is a boy we will name him Salvatore after you, the man who saved my life, " he said with devotion.

As Salvo listened to this outpouring of love, a tear came to his eye.

"If it is a girl," he whispered, "will you name her Theresa?"

"Yes! We will have many children and I promise you that our first girl will be named Theresa! It would be our honor to give her a name chosen by you!" the boy exclaimed. He was genuinely joyful to do anything for Salvo.

Daniel continued to sit by Salvo's bedside. He would tell him the news of the war, the whereabouts of their surviving combat brothers, and what Salvo had gone through while he was unconscious. He told him how his perception of the world had shifted while preparing himself to be Salvo's eyes, and how he thanked God every day for restoring his sight. There was a power in Daniel's sensitivity that animated his voice and body. Salvo saw that he communicated from the purity of his soul. He reminded him of the boy he once was: the boy from the Collegio Romano, who loved to sing the holy songs, and pray for peace. Sometimes as he was falling asleep at night, it gave Salvo comfort to think that if he and Theresa had a son, he would have been like Daniel.

One afternoon, as the boy sat at his bedside telling him the news of the war, Salvo was suddenly overwhelmed with the memory of all the battles he had fought in. The horrific images of nihilism, suffering, and carnage unfolded in his mind causing him to urgently interrupt the boy.

"You mustn't blame yourself for what happened on the battlefield," he began. Your reaction to the death and violence of that day was not an act of cowardice. It was an act of sanity. You reacted as a decent and loving man bearing witness to cruelty and destruction so evil that no sane human could accept it. You must never blame yourself for what happened to me. I do not blame you. I thank you. I was lost in a nightmare. I could no longer endure life or the living. I sought out death and the dying. I chose war as my constant companion. In saving you a new path opened to me, a path that led me out of despair. I want to live again. That has been your gift to me. Promise me that you will carry no burden of guilt, shame or self-doubt. Promise me that you will embrace life and know the joy contained in the goodness of your soul. Let that be my gift to you."

A weight was lifted from Daniel's heart. The room seemed to become much brighter. Daniel could only nod his head in agreement. And with the absolution of this boy, Salvo's desire for his own destruction ended.

Shortly after that afternoon the boy, no longer useful in battle, received his orders to return to his home in France. It was time to say goodbye. The boy wanted to keep in touch to tell Salvo of the birth of his child. They exchanged their information. The boy held Salvo's hand and just looked at him, his gaze overflowing with love. This tragedy had changed him. His selfless love for Salvo had introduced him to his destiny. Later, on the train, he would begin to sketch: documenting the sights around him in great detail with his newly trained eyes. And then after a few years he would begin to paint the French countryside of his home. Eventually he would become a renowned artist. But at this moment he did not know what awaited him. There was only the sadness of parting with his dearest friend, who had forgiven him when he could not forgive himself.

"If not for you, my wife would be a widow and my child fatherless. I can never repay you," he said.

"You loved me when I did not love myself," Salvo began. "You brought me back into the land of the living. Be a good man. Be a good husband and father. I will think of you and your family often and be very happy," Salvo replied.

There was nothing more to say. Daniel turned and left.

Now that Salvo was alone, he thought about the extent of his injuries. The doctors told him that his blindness had been temporary and would not return. However, his throat and lungs had been severely damaged. He knew that he would never sing again.

It was now close to the end of October 1918, and he was anticipating receiving orders to leave the hospital. He was lying quietly in his bed thinking about where he might go when he received an unexpected visitor. A very handsome Naval Officer stood at his bedside. There was an instant recognition that both men felt although they knew they had never met. The officer was carrying a package, which he placed on the bedside table.

"May I sit down?" the officer asked.

"Of course," Salvo whispered still barely able to speak.

"My name is Robert," the officer began.

Salvo knew his name was Robert before he told him.

"You are Theresa's brother," Salvo whispered.

"Yes," Robert began. "Did she speak of me?"

"Often, and with great love," Salvo answered.

"We share a great sadness," Robert said.

"Yes," Salvo whispered. A tear came to his eye.

"And a great love," Robert added.

Salvo searched his eyes wanting to know more.

"My Father told me about your love and your plans to marry," Robert continued.

Salvo could only nod.

"I was injured in the Straits of Gibraltar and was sent home to recover with my family in Wisconsin. I was there when I received the news of my sister's death. And then my father arrived with her body. "

Robert stopped for a moment. He took a deep breath and continued.

"She was surrounded by her family and friends when she was buried. The whole town was there. She was deeply loved by everyone. We were all so proud of her. I thought you would want to know."

Again Robert stopped, too consumed with grief to speak. They sat in silence for a short while. When Robert could go on, he continued.

"My father told me how he sat with you in Paris, at Theresa's bedside. He told me how devoted you were to one another. I loved my sister with all my heart. I am comforted knowing that she had found love with you in the brief time she was here with us. I wish things could have turned out differently."

Robert broke down and wept. Salvo and he both wept. Again they sat in silence. After a while Robert continued.

"When we tried to contact you we found out that you had volunteered to join the army. My father and I tracked you down and discovered that you were on the Sinai Peninsula. When I received my orders to return to service I was assigned to duty in the Suez Canal. So I promised my family that I would find you. We want you to know that we will always be your family if you need us. And we decided that we wanted you to have this."

Robert lifted the heavy package off the table. Salvo reached out for it. As they both held it, Salvo knew what it was. It was the book of sacred music. At this moment both men felt like they had experienced this before. Time slipped away and there was only the two of them sharing a profound love, a deep sadness and a regenerating trust each in the other.

"Shall I open it for you?" Robert asked.

"Yes, please," Salvo replied.

The string and paper slipped away revealing the book that had meant so much to all of them. Robert opened it to the cover page where Theresa had sketched the portrait of Salvo. Salvo read the words she had written, "Love is eternal, and eternity is now."

"This is why we thought that you must have this book," Robert explained.

"Yes," Salvo whispered. "Thank you".

What he thought would be unbearable pain at the remembrance of this day was somehow changed by Robert's presence. Salvo wept with gratitude as he held the book to his heart. But still he couldn't bear the memory of anything more.

Robert visited several more times before he had to return to his ship. He told Salvo of the gull, the white bird that had come to save him after the torpedo attack. He shared what the Sardinian fishermen had told him of their vision, and how Theresa's parting gift to him was the unification of his body and soul. Robert confided to Salvo that his father had been greatly changed when he returned from Paris. That he had been a deeply troubled man, violent and unable to love or to even communicate with his family. But when he returned from Paris he had become loving, even effusive with all he wanted his family to know about the many years he had withheld his love from them.

Salvo, in turn, told Robert of his friendship with the young boy that had lost his mind on the battlefield, and the child that would be named after Theresa. Their communications were very intense and meaningful. But Salvo still could not speak of his time with Theresa. It was locked away and only acknowledged by an agonizing emptiness that could not yet be approached.

Robert helped Salvo to make plans for his release from the hospital. He would return to Italy to spend time with his family. Once there he would find work of some kind. After their talks they would sit in silence just wanting to be in each other's presence.

When Robert had to return to his ship for duty they parted as those who know they will never be parted. His friendship had changed Salvo's life. Robert had somehow introduced Salvo to the man the tragedies he had suffered had made him. He had shown him that he was a man imminently worth knowing. Now Salvo had a renewed sense of purpose.

13

Salvo returned to Italy to find that the entire world was in the grips of a second wave of the Spanish Flu. This one was far more deadly than the first. It was now recognized as a pandemic. People were dying by the tens of thousands. All were being told to quarantine and to wear face coverings when they had to leave their homes. By the grace of God his parents and sisters had not fallen sick with it. He learned from the letters his brothers sent that they had all survived the war, thus far, with only minor injuries. Salvo's injuries were the most severe. The money he had made during his singing career was enough to sustain the family for a long time. Then, only days after he had arrived home, on November 11, 1918, Germany's ruler, Kaiser Wilhelm, having been told by his military leaders that he could not win the war, stepped down. The war ended and all of Salvo's brothers returned home. The family was counting their blessings that they were all together again. Their great sadness was that Salvo's injuries had taken away his angelic voice and left him to speak in a raspy whisper. But he would have none of it.

"Be grateful that I am alive and that we are all here together again," he would tell them. "We are very blessed. So many did not come home and many did not have loving families to welcome them home."

Although the pandemic was still raging, training centers were set up to train the returning soldiers in new skills to support them in their new civilian lives. By the beginning of 1919 Salvo's brothers had selected new professions and were learning the skills needed to become cobblers and jewelers. Salvo spent his time in prayer. Being home with his family brought back memories of his boyhood, and his desire to become a priest. He studied the book of sacred music and heard it clearly in his head. Even as he sang these songs silently, he was connected to the sacred realms encoded on the pages. What had once been instinctive was now conscious understanding. His connection to music became even greater.

Now, in February of 1919, as a third wave of the Spanish Flu was sweeping through the world, with his face carefully covered as mandated, and the book of sacred music under his arm, Salvo made his way to his beloved seminary. In 1913 the seminary where he had studied had merged with another institution to become *The Pontifico Seminario Romano Minore.*

He stood outside of the gates. He was uncertain. He felt unworthy to enter. A vocation that was once as natural as breathing was now complicated and riddled with conflict. Would they accept him, a man who had been a soldier? A man who had lived a very public, secular life?

He thought of the innocence with which his vocation had come to him as a boy. There was no question that his calling to serve God was authentic. Would he have been a better servant of the Lord if he had continued on this path uninterrupted by the intrusion of life, a life not of his choosing, but one that had been forced upon him by misfortune? It had taught him what it meant to have his family fractured, and to have his path redirected from a world of perfect trust and union to a world where obedience and devotion were demanded by the rich to make them richer. He had learned how to make music, once only known to him as holy, into an amusement to attract the attention of those who would pay him. He learned how to use his voice in the service of high art, enabling the masses to experience transcendence, and he, himself, to become rich. He had learned through his friendships that there are many paths to God, and many ways to be of service defined in many different ways. He had stood in the blinding spotlight and excited lust in the bodies of women and adulation in the thousands who listened to him sing. He had voluntarily offered himself into the service of his country to engage in warfare against his fellow man to preserve a way of life believed to be righteous. He had sacrificed himself to save one young boy, whose gratitude and devotion reawakened his heart when all was lost. He had watched a father's heart burst open with love for his estranged daughter, and had experienced an unexpected fraternal love with her brother, so binding that it healed his soul and gave him the will to go on living. But most of all, he had loved a woman so deeply that when he lost her he couldn't find his way in the darkness that was the world without her illuminating his way.

He stood there outside of the gates for hours, remembering everything about her that had been mercifully blocked from him until he could withstand the loss that accompanied the memory. He studied the portrait she had drawn of him on the cover page of the book he carried. He saw it as if for the first time, with a deeper comprehension of who she was and what she was expressing. Grief had lifted the curtain of illusion and anything that had separated them in life was now absent. He looked at the pencil lines so thin that they were more of a thread: a thread so fragile that it could barely contain the space within it. He understood that her soul had always been contained by the thinnest of earthly membranes. That was her gift. She was more spirit than flesh. The two of them, imperfect as they were, had lived in a spiritual universe obtainable only by the truest of loves. His heart swelled with gratitude at the blessing he had been granted. The bottomless well of grief that he had been living in now became a bottomless well of love. There was no end to it. He was shown how deeply he could love and how, unlike the thin lines that contain us, that love is indestructible. He knew with certainty that he, nor anyone else, is ever alone, and that no room is ever empty.

He was still outside the seminary gates when the seminarians began their Vesper prayers. As if to send him a welcoming message they began to sing *Salve Regina.*

Although sung by men, he could hear Theresa's voice coming to him, through time, or maybe it came from all around him. It joined with the men's choir to welcome him home:

"Triumph, all ye Cherubim
Sing with us, ye Seraphim
Heaven and earth resound the hymn,
Salve, salve, salve Regina!"

Sure of himself now, and with a full heart, he left the past with all its guilt and conflict behind. He took a deep renewing breath and walked through the gates of the seminary into the embrace of his destiny.

Salvo's days as a seminarian were lived with humility, joy, gratitude and service, as if it each day was his last. When he was ordained to the priesthood he took the name Father Michael. He heard from Robert and Claude often and they even came to visit him while traveling abroad. On one special trip Claude and Robert brought their families to Italy to meet him. Claude introduced Salvo to his wife Greta. Robert introduced him to his wife Gwendolyn. They now had three daughters, Katherine, Rebecca and Amy. The girls were giddy with excitement to meet Salvo, whom they had heard so much about. They loved him immediately and considered him to be a part of their family. It was on this trip that Robert took Salvo aside to talk to him privately. Salvo had noticed that Robert was very pale, thin and gaunt, so he had anticipated what Robert had come to tell him. He had been infected with Malaria while on duty in the Suez Canal. He had never fully recovered and had suffered relapses over the years. Lately they had become more severe, threatening his life. He was growing weak and didn't have much time left. This would be the last time they would see each other. He had come to say goodbye. They embraced each other, with the knowledge that their journey together had come to an end. Then they stood close, looking deeply into one another's eyes. Robert spoke first.

"I leave with a full heart", he said quietly.

"My cup runneth over", Salvo answered.

Robert turned and walked quietly away.

Soon afterwards, Daniel traveled from France to Italy to visit Salvo. He had made a good life for his family as a farmer and was gaining recognition as an artist for his masterful depictions of the French countryside. He brought with him his wife and their children, Salvo and Theresa. They had been told about the origin of their names and how Salvo had saved their father's life in the war. Upon meeting Salvo they wept. But their tears were short lived as they delighted in the love and good humor with which he greeted them. They owed their very life to him. He would always be a part of their family.

His voice had healed enough for him to be able to chant the Latin liturgy as he officiated at Mass. But he knew that his lungs had been severely damaged and that he would not live a long life.

He lived long enough to witness the rise of Hitler and the Third Reich. He acted under direct orders from Pope Pius XII assisting the Jews in escaping the death camps, and in hiding the Allied Forces from the Nazis. Having been in the army Salvo had experienced tyranny and brutality. He was not intimidated or made confused by the bombardment of the Nazi persecutors when they came to search the churches and question the priests at gunpoint. He taught those in his community how to approach their daunting, life and death responsibilities with effective strategic planning and a cool head in the service of divine providence. With the help of the Catholic priests and nuns, tens of thousands of Jews and soldiers were saved.

On September 2, 1945, the war finally ended. Days later Salvo collapsed after officiating at a Baptism. He was taken to what he knew would be his deathbed. He was fifty years old. He had been suffering from lung cancer for several years, but he had endured the pain silently and was always at the ready to be of service where needed. He suffered in those final days. When he knew the end was near he asked to be given the Last Rites.

Afterwards his fellow priests were called to Vespers. One stayed behind to tend to him, sitting outside the door to his room, which was left open, so that he could hear his brothers singing. As he listened, he could feel Theresa near him. His breathing was labored now and the pain severe. She took away his pain with the caresses of a gentle breeze, and soothed him with the warmth of her glowing countenance, which hovered over him, bringing him closer and closer into the light. As the holy music filled the room, he felt her lips upon his, and he dissolved into her kiss, ascending, knowing that his work on earth was completed. He let go of this world and became one with her in eternity.

When Vespers ended it was discovered that he had passed over. The priests from his community gathered around his bed to pay their last respects and to pray for his soul. Some were saddened thinking that he died alone, in an empty room. Others, more finely tuned, could feel the presence of the angelic realm all around him. And some could hear, in the angelic frequency, the singing of a man and a woman so perfectly blended that it was the song of one soul.

PART THREE

WRITING WITH LIGHT

Chicago: 1970's

1

Michael poured himself a glass of bitter lemon. His father had been an alcoholic so he never drank liquor. He walked into the living room of his house, a small "fixer upper" in an unfashionable neighborhood on the West Side of Chicago. He sat in his comfortable chair, near the front window to keep vigil. He watched the storm. The wind had picked up and the rain was coming down in buckets. He was worried about Marissa. As he sipped his drink, he smiled a sensual smile remembering the first time he had ever laid eyes on her. It was only a photograph, an actor's head shot that he had been handed, but she was so present he could taste her. He had a sixth sense. This had given him a reputation as a reliable detective in the Chicago PD.

Some said he was psychic, but he paid no attention to things like that. He lived in the real world. Along with most of the young men of his generation he had been drafted and sent to fight in the Vietnam War. He served his two years as a squad leader in infantry. Afterwards he volunteered for the Peace Corps and spent two years in Panama. When he returned to his hometown of Berwyn he became a cop. He had some bad experiences with corrupt individuals, motivating him, after a few years, to use the money he had saved to buy his house on the West Side. Now he was a detective working a North Side area. He had seen the worst of what human beings were capable of. Even so, beneath his sarcasm and dark humor, he remained a compassionate and tolerant man. His devout Irish Catholic parents had named him Michael, after the archangel. But everyone called him Mickey.

It was a Saturday in early September of 1976. He had been on duty since 4 p.m. It was a slow day. Around 8:30 p.m., just as he was about to eat an Italian sausage sandwich, a report came in from a patrol officer requesting a detective. His sergeant dispatched him to a Rogers Park apartment. It was hers. He wolfed down a few bites of the sandwich then stuffed it back into its bag and threw it down on the seat next to him. He was not happy.

She lived on a short side street off of Sheridan Road. Her street ended in a cul-de-sac, on the shore of Lake Michigan. She lived in a three-story brick building with a courtyard, long stone balconies and lots of tall windows. The gutters were made from copper, which had oxidized over the years, making them green. There was a fountain in the courtyard depicting a young boy sheltering a young girl with an umbrella. It hadn't worked in decades. It was one of those old buildings that cast a spell. It had the European aesthetics of a bygone era, which invoked a pleasing feeling of nostalgia.

The heavy wood and glass vestibule door, usually locked, was held open by a cinder block in anticipation of his arrival. Taped to the door was a note that read: 'Marissa's Viewing Party Canceled Until Further Notice. Sorry.'

As he walked up the winding stairs to the third floor, he noticed that the building was crooked. One side had sunk into the soft sandy ground closest to the lake. Peculiarities like this made these spacious apartments from the glory days of Rogers Park reasonable to rent. Once only the wealthy lived here. Now it was the part of Chicago where you could get the most bang for your buck.

When he entered her apartment, his first impression was that it looked like a stage set. It was dramatic. Each piece of vintage furniture had been carefully chosen and positioned for its visual impact. Nothing matched, but the montage of animal-prints, brocades, velvet, needlepoint and carved wood all complemented each other in a stunning way. There were vintage mirrors everywhere. The large ornate ones hung over the fireplace and on the walls. The ones too large to hang, stood against the walls and the small ones rested on easels that were placed on the coffee table, the bar, and shelves. The tall windows were open and the filmy white curtains were blowing in the breeze. They wafted about in a billowy dance that was fitting to the ambiance of the room. In the dining room there was a large screen set up, blocking the windows, which would have faced the alley, and lighting equipment cluttered the floor. The young patrol officer approached him.

"Whatcha got kid?" Mickey asked.

He was handed a photograph, a "head shot". The kind submitted by actors at an audition. The name 'Marissa' was in bold black letters across the bottom. His response was immediate. Her looks stirred him as a man. She was pretty. She had striking gray eyes, well-defined features and long dark hair. He could feel her intensity. Warm pulses of electricity flowed through him as he looked at her. She didn't have the usual mandatory vapid smile of an actress. She was serious and focused. Her image flooded his senses. He was interrupted by the officer.

"Excuse me detective, this is her neighbor Paul. He lives across the hall. He's the one that reported her missing. "

"Hi," he replied. "Call me Mickey."

As they shook hands Mickey assessed him. He was a bright, quirky young man, beaming with energy and inventiveness. His eyes were guileless and his manner straightforward and friendly. He was wearing a cut off sweatshirt with the word "I T A L I A" on the front.

Mickey focused his uncompromising gaze on him and began his interrogation.

"How do you know Marissa?"

"We met for the first time when I moved in. We were friends right away. We've been friends and neighbors for a few years," Paul replied. Then he added, "Nothing more."

"Did you move here from Italia?" Mickey asked indicating Paul's sweatshirt.

"Naw," he replied. "That's just someplace I've always wanted to go."

"What makes you think Marissa's missing?"

"Early this afternoon I heard knocking on her door. I thought something wasn't right, because we have to buzz people in the downstairs door. I looked through my peephole and saw a tall blonde guy standing there...but I only saw his back. I wondered how he got in. Then I thought she must have buzzed him in, but not been waiting for him at the door, so I let it go. She was having a video screening of her latest gig tonight, and I was coming over early to help her set up. I saw that her door was open so I called out to her but there was no answer. That was about four hours ago. I waited for her to come home, but she never did."

"Maybe she's running late. Maybe she had to go out and forgot to close her door," Mickey replied, peeved that his dinner was shot because some broad forgot to shut her door.

"She was expecting a bunch of people here at 7:30. And she wouldn't have left her door open even if she had left," Paul explained. "She has a cat."

"Where's the cat now?"

"In my apartment. I didn't want it to get scared so I took it to my place. Was that okay? Did I do something wrong?"

"No, you did right," Mickey replied. He liked the kid. Besides it saved him the trouble of calling Animal Control.

"I'll go get her," Paul said as he hurried across the hall into his apartment.

"Are there any security cameras in this joint?" Mickey asked the officer.

"Naw," he answered. "That's the problem with these old buildings. No doorman, no security system..." he was interrupted by the neighbor rushing back in with a dainty gray cat in his arms.

"This is her cat, Morgan le Fay. Marissa never would have left the door open with Morgan here," he said earnestly. "And she would have been here on time to greet her guests. When people started to arrive I sent them home and put a note on the downstairs door that it had been canceled. I waited another hour and then I called the police".

"Is that it?" Mickey impatiently asked, shifting his focus to the officer.

"No. There's this," the patrol officer said indicating an antique *étagère* in the corner of the room. They walked over and stood in front of it. It held a collection of crystal objects. They looked expensive. On the floor nearby was a smashed figurine.

"This was her collection of Lalique crystal," Paul told Mickey. "That was a Lalique bird."

Mickey knelt on the floor to look at the broken pieces. "This is heavy crystal," he remarked. "It would have to be thrown down with a lot of force to shatter like that." He knew she hadn't smashed it. Her captor had.

'Tell him what you told me," the officer instructed Paul.

"For the last week we have been finding birds, with their heads cut off, outside our building by the fountain. A few of us filed police reports if you want to look it up."

"Did you see anyone hanging around the building?" Mickey asked.

"No, but I'm thinking that maybe the guy I saw at her door...I don't know."

"Had you ever seen him before?"

"I only saw his back, so I don't know. I don't think so."

"There's more", said the officer. "Come with me,"

The officer led Mickey into the bathroom. Written in soap on the glass shower door was the letter "L".

"She wrote on the glass door instead of the mirror so he couldn't see it," Mickey thought. "Good thinking."

As Mickey examined the writing he noted that a lot of pressure had been put on the soap. It had been scrawled with haste by a panicked hand. Her fear flashed through him. She had dropped the soap on the floor. She was interrupted. He examined it. It was dry and there was a blunted spot on one end. She had been taken hours ago. He smelled it. Lavender.

"She probably has trouble sleeping," he thought.

"One more thing," the officer continued, as he brought Mickey over to the VHS machine set up in the dining room near the screen. "This was turned on but the tape hasn't been played. It would need to be re-wound if it had been."

Mickey pushed a button on the VHS and music began to play. It was *Dream Lover*. Not the rock and roll version by Ricky Nelson, but the old composition by Victor Schertzinger and Clifford Gray. Mickey had heard it before as soundtrack on very old movies. Now, as it played, Marissa appeared in a ball gown. It was from another era. He had seen gowns like this when he had been dragged to the opera by the women in his life. It had a full skirt and a fitted bodice made of purple, gold and silver fabric. Mickey was strangely moved by the sight of her in that dress. As she moved to the center of what looked to be a ballroom he was surprised to see that she was transparent! She was a hologram!

"I didn't see that coming," he said jokingly as they all chuckled, breaking the tension. The three of them watched attentively. They were intrigued.

Marissa began to sing in a clear, pitch-perfect soprano voice, as she danced gracefully across the dance floor.

"Dream lover, fold your arms around me
Dream lover, your romance has found me
I'm held in your spell
Knowing so well, dreams never tell."

While she performed, projected images of famous lovers from the movies danced on screens, which lined the perimeter of the space, even onto the ceiling. The effect was a cocoon of romance that the audience was invited into. Sometimes the images of the movie stars would move into close ups as they twirled in each other's arms, and then explode into light, like fireworks, as others took their place. Sometimes all of their images filled the screens, dancing, swirling around Marissa as she sang with outstretched arms, beckoning the audience to dance with her. One brave young man started the ball rolling. He stepped forward and danced with her as the room went wild with applause. Then others took his place. Soon everyone, male and female, was eager to dance with her holographic image. Eventually everyone came onto the ballroom floor to join her and the screen lovers, dancing with each other until the whole ballroom was filled with dancers. It was very captivating, even to the hardened police officers. When it ended they were silent for a moment. They too had been transported into this dream world of Marissa's creation. None of them had ever seen anything like this before. It was the seventies. Holograms and video projections were still fairly new. Not many artists were working in this medium because it was almost impossible to get grant money, or investors interested, because it didn't fit into any known category.

"She's a performance artist. Her medium is holograms," Paul told them. "She told me that years ago she developed her pieces in art friendly university labs in San Francisco. She was part of the Haight-Ashbury scene. She performed at a few specialty hologram museums there before moving back to Chicago to be near her family. Here in Chicago she does commissioned parties. She has a cult following. They call her "Marissa".

"Isn't that her name?" Mickey asked.

"Yeah, that's her name," Paul answered. Then he added, "She told me that her name was really Mary Theresa, but she thought it sounded like a medieval nun. So when she grew up she combined the two names together to make it 'Marissa'."

A fleeting image of her as a medieval nun flashed through Mickey's mind. But it was gone before he could fully realize it.

Mickey looked at the cover of the VHS tape. The label said, "Recorded at The Fantasy Prom." It was dated a few weeks ago.

"What's a Fantasy Prom?" Mickey asked Paul with a tone of mockery.

"It's a big shindig for people who never got to go to a prom or didn't like the ones they went to. The gay community started them, but they caught on and now everyone goes. Marissa is a big attraction."

"Do you go to these?"

"I can't afford it," he explained. "I'm just a poor graphic artist. Marissa has viewing parties for us poor people," he said with a laugh. "Like the one I was invited to tonight."

Mickey got it. The captor had told her he had come for the viewing, pretending to have mixed up the time. That's why she let him in.

"I'm gonna take a look around," he said as he headed into Marissa's bedroom.

There on the door in a dry-cleaning bag was the ball gown from the video. He took it from the bag and examined it. He felt like he had touched it before. It was very old and the bodice had been patched and repaired many times. Many of the gold, silver and purple threads were broken and hanging loose. To him they were like little electrical wires buzzing with information. If only they had a mechanism for language...

the stories they could tell! The gown had an old, yellowed label from a costume shop in Paris. He could smell her perfume, and beyond that, her scent. He saw her in his mind's eye dancing in this dress. But it was in a different place, in a different time.

Her bedroom furniture was also vintage. On her carved dressing table she had many bottles of perfume: Chanel, Bulgari, Guerlain, Nina Ricci, Yves Saint Laurent...all classics...none of the trendy scents.

"She's a collector," he thought.

She had vintage lamps, Dresden figurines, music books, anthologies of plays...lots of stuff. Again, everything was placed in a special way for visual impact rather than for ease of use. He opened her closet door. The smell of perfume and leather filled his lungs. It was a large walk-in closet containing clothing, shoes, handbags and hatboxes. He pulled out a few pieces of clothing. They too were unique. They weren't expensive designer labels, but each piece was a little work of art. He looked at a silk blouse with an abstract blue and green pattern. He saw the park on a summer's day, humming with happy, noisy activity. There was a white peasant blouse made of a silky eyelet fabric. It was like holding a cloud. He examined a velvet blouse with a design cut into it, possibly by a laser. It reminded him of music: a Frank Sinatra tune that came to him in bits and pieces, only half remembered:

"Dressed in dreams for me...
make believe was coming true...
dressed in memories, you are what you used to be..."

He struggled to remember more of the lyrics, but the intrusion of his conscious mind made the song fade away, leaving behind it only a vague feeling of frustration.

The clothes were in mint condition but the labels were all old and faded.

"She shops at thrift stores," he thought. "Everything is chosen to elicit a mood and to encourage non-verbal communication."

There was a collection of artwork on her bedroom walls. They were vintage lithographs: French poster art. He noticed the way they were hung and laughed to himself. To the observant viewer she was telling the story of a girl progressing through life. The girl lived in many different dream-like spaces, amidst many hues of colors. She walked in the sun. Animals were her companions. She found friendship, sexual power, transcendence, drama, fame, grief, treachery and betrayal. And then in the final lithograph she became the author of her journey. The image was that of a barefoot girl with long, loose black hair, dressed as a goddess. She was in profile, holding up a magnifying glass to a light source and projecting the light onto a blank piece of paper, which she held in her hand. The poster read: "Writing with Light." Mickey was getting to know her.

He walked out onto the balcony. He listened to the sounds of the traffic on Sheridan Road. As he listened, they blended together sounding like a frenetic urban jazz composition. He looked at the roof across the courtyard. It was covered with crescent-shaped *terra cotta* tiles and small stone chimneys. Each chimney was carved in a different whimsical design. He thought about the care and artistry that went into constructing this building. He could hear the movement of Lake Michigan within its shores. Its enormous force spoke to him in a quiet, rolling roar, sometimes ebbing and then growing quiet, but never silent. He put aside his knowledge of what tragedies lie hidden beneath its surface and thought, "How nice it must be to lie in bed and listen to the lake."

He returned to the living room. This was her public space where friends and colleagues gathered. Again he laughed to himself. He got it. Rather than hanging artwork in here she had hung mirrors. The reflection of whoever was in the room was the artwork. It was a life affirming gesture, always current and endlessly fascinating. He looked at himself in a large ornate mirror on the wall. It hung at a slight angle. The framing and the background surrounding his image made him see himself differently. It wasn't anything he could explain. He felt like he was trying to remember something. As he studied his reflection, the reflection of something else caught his eye. On a small table by the door there was a spyglass. He walked over to the table. The spyglass was set on top of a business card that read, "Kooky Karaoke." He knew at once it was another deliberate message left by her.

"She knew she was being abducted," he thought. "She knew her captor."

"Hey Paul," he called out. "Do you like to sing Karaoke?"

"Oh God, no!" Paul answered. "Not my thing. I hate those places."

Mickey located Marissa's phone and dialed the number on the card. He found out that Kooky Karaoke was set up at a nearby bar.

"Okay, file your report. Put my name on it, and then lock it up," he told the patrol officer. Waving the card he added, "I'm going down the street to check out this bar." He left hurriedly.

It was an old neighborhood bar, nothing special, except for the generations of neighborhood friends that met there. It was nothing like the new upscale bars downtown that catered to the yuppies and the "too cool for school" hipsters. The walls were covered with photos of patrons, some of whom had gone on to become celebrities. Mickey noticed one of some of the improvisers from Second City, an iconic Chicago comedy club he frequented. There were many of up and coming Chicago actors, and among them there was an autographed photo of Marissa.

A great big, baby-faced disk jockey sat fielding requests behind a utility table surrounded by karaoke gear. It was around 10 p.m. It was still early for a bar, but a crowd had already gathered. A young man and woman were laughing their way through *You're The One That I Want* while the others happily ordered drinks and excitedly greeted one and other,

Mickey approached the DJ and flashed his badge. The DJ looked scared.

"He's got marijuana in his pocket," Mickey thought.

He asked him if he could talk to him. The DJ agreed to take a break once this number ended. His frightened look relaxed as Mickey pointed to the photo of Marissa and asked if he knew her.

"Oh yeah, Marissa," he began. "She's one of our favorites! She comes in all the time!"

"When was the last time you saw her?"

"She was in last week."

"Was she alone?"

"No. She always comes in with friends. The 'artsy' crowd. But they are all pretty nice, and they tip well."

"Did anything unusual happen? Did anybody bother her?"

"This is a bar. Men are always bothering women trying to pick them up. You know."

"Was someone trying to pick up Marissa?"

"No...well...not pick her up. But there is this one guy who always wants to sing with her."

"What does he look like?"

"He's tall, blonde, very handsome, like a movie star or something."

"What's his name?"

"I don't remember...wait...Lou...it might be Lou."

"Does she sing with him?"

"Yeah, she's real nice to everyone. She'll sing with anyone who asks her. But this guy wants to sing with her all the time. Every time she comes in. He's kind of a pain in the ass, but he's got a great voice. All the chicks dig him. They come here looking for him. He's good for business so we leave him alone."

"What songs do they sing together?"

"They sing *Dream A Little Dream Of Me*, or *All I Have To Do Is Dream*. Last week he wanted to sing *Goodnight, Irene*.

Mickey knew that song. It was an oldie that ends, "Goodnight

Irene, Goodnight Irene, I'll see you in my dreams." A chill ran through Mickey.

"Does he ever sing alone?" Mickey asked.

"Yeah," the DJ answered. "He likes to sing *I Will Follow You.*"

Mickey knew.

This was the guy. "L" for Lou. He likes to play games. He's a trickster. He continued with his interrogation.

"Is he a regular? Does he live in the neighborhood?"

"I don't know. I've never noticed him hanging out with anyone else. Like I said, he's a real handsome guy so a lot of the chicks come on to him. But I've never seen him leave with any of them. In fact he blows them off. He just comes in and wants to sing with Marissa. Oh...and he likes to play that video game 'Death Race.'" He gestured to a console against the wall. "If she's not here he plays for hours. It pisses people off."

"Has she ever left with him?"

"I don't think so. She always leaves with her friends. Sometimes they invite me to go have something to eat at Tempo or some other late night joint. But I can't leave the equipment in the truck out on the street. My boss would kill me."

"Are there any photos of him on the wall?"

"There is probably a photo of him singing with Marissa up there. The owner is always taking pictures. Jeez, we have pictures on the wall from 30 years ago."

Michael scoured the wall for more photos of Marissa. He found a few, but they were from a distance. Then he saw one of her singing on the tiny stage with a tall, good-looking guy who was staring at her with an unnatural intensity. Then he found another with the same guy watching her from across the room with the same intensity. He pulled the photos off the wall.

"Is this the guy?" Mickey asked.

"Yeah, that's him."

"Did you ever hear him talking to her about anything?"

"Only to ask her to sing. She always went right back to her friends afterwards. But, you know, I do remember that the owner threw him out once. He came in with a concealed gun. "

"When was this?"

"A while back: maybe a month ago. But I heard him say he had a permit and he carried it because he was going to the "Cowboy Bar" later. The owner made him leave and told him not to bring his gun in here again."

Mickey knew all about the Cowboy Bar. It was on the West Side not far from where he lived. Most people avoided it like the plague. It was a wild place and a thorn in the side of local law enforcement. It catered to a hardcore, gun-carrying crowd of bikers, radicals, wannabe cowboys and a subculture of small-time criminals. It also attracted a following of weekend warriors who were looking for a walk on the wild side. One Saturday a month, as the night progressed and they all got drunk, the patrons would shoot into the tin ceiling at the stroke of midnight. The small attic space above had been sealed off for decades and nothing was up there but rats.

"Oh yeah, The Cowboy Bar, there's a lot of beefs about that place," Mickey said to the DJ, watching for his reaction. "The owner's a scumbag, but heavier than whale shit. He's an untouchable. So the place never gets shut down."

"Not my kind of place. I've heard a few stories but I've never been there." The DJ replied.

Mickey believed him.

"Is the owner here?" Mickey asked the DJ.

"He doesn't come in until after eleven."

"How can I reach him?"

"You can call him, but he won't answer. He never does. Believe me I speak from experience," the DJ said as he wrote down the number on a napkin.

Mickey tried calling the owner of the bar from the pay phone on the wall, but as the DJ had warned, he didn't answer. It didn't matter. He had enough information to go on. As the coins clattered into the coin return he gathered them up and reinserted them into the slot. He called the police district where the Cowboy Bar was.

"Give me Tact", he said. "Hey Sarge it's Mickey."

"Whatcha got?" asked the Sergeant.

"I'm doing follow up on a case at the Cowboy Bar," Mickey began.

"That shithole!" the Sergeant exclaimed.

"Yeah, that joint. You got anyone in soft clothes that can back me up tonight?"

"I got Garza and Fogel."

"Not those two fuck ups!"

"That's what they say about you asshole."

"Naw, I was just kidding. They're good. I've worked with them before."

"Fogel is right here. Tell him whatcha got."

"Hey Fogel, I gotta talk to some guy at the Cowboy Bar. He's supposed to be kinky. Can you and Garza sit at the bar and back me up?"

"See you there," was all Fogel said.

Mickey hung up and checked the coin return. No luck.

He wanted to check out the video games before he left. Some college kids were playing "Tank". He watched them as they maneuvered controls, howling with laughter as they blew each other up. He moved on to the game "Death Race". It was a solitary game. It was operated by a steering wheel, which the player controlled as he ran down his victims, then murdered them. For an instant he felt Lou's energy. He entered into Lou's mind. As he played, he would repeat part of a Bible verse. Mickey knew from his Jesuit education that it was Peter 5:8

"...the Devil walks about like a roaring Lion,
seeking whom he may devour".

Mickey got it. "Lou" wants to be Lucifer.

"If this guy Lou comes in here tonight call this number immediately," Mickey instructed the DJ as he handed him his card. "Tell them it's Mickey's case. Can I take these photos with me?" he asked. It was a perfunctory question. He would have taken them anyway.

"Sure. No problem," the DJ replied, feeling cool because he was aiding in an investigation. "If you go to the Cowboy Bar, I wouldn't let anyone know you're a cop," the DJ added. "They might tip him off."

"Oh yeah! Good thinking," Mickey said feigning surprise. "I would have never thought of that."

He hated advice from amateurs. But he did appreciate that the DJ cared, so he didn't ask to see the contents of his pocket.

He made his way to the Cowboy Bar through the Saturday night traffic. It was the "Swinging Seventies", and the streets were packed with college kids from Loyola out for a good time. He was distracted by the girls in their mini skirts and platform shoes as groups of them sashayed down the Sheridan Road sidewalks. They were bold, non-compliant, and didn't answer to men. "The Sexual Revolution" was in full swing and not many denied themselves the experience of their own sexuality. Propriety was a thing of the past.

He thought about the women in his life. He had been engaged twice: once to a girl from the West Side, and once to a girl from the North Side. The only thing they had in common was that they both wanted to reform him. They both told him he lacked sensitivity. They said he was a male chauvinist. They wanted to take him to EST and transcendental meditation and sensitivity training. It was a shock to them to find out that he thought he was just fine the way he was.

"You'll never change," they said.

They were right. He didn't want to change. They just didn't get him.

"Oh well, what the hell," he thought. "There are plenty of other women in the world."

He turned on the radio. A Beatles tune was playing. The Fab Four sang out in their penetrating harmony:

"And it really doesn't matter if I'm wrong or right
Where I belong I'm right, where I belong."

Mickey thought about his failed relationships. He thought about his life and the times he had been an outcast, through no fault of his own, but just because he didn't belong there, and he thought, "There's a lot of wisdom in those lyrics".

It was a little past 11:30 p.m. when he arrived at the bar. The boisterous noise of the crowd was spilling out onto the streets. But there was no sound of gunfire yet.

"The fun will be starting soon," he thought.

He parked on a side street about a block away, took off his trench coat, suit coat and tie and put on the denim jacket he kept in his truck. He went into the alley behind the bar and looked around. There were a few cars parked there and some trashcans. Some rats scurried by. An old tree with a thick trunk was flush up against the side of the building. He walked around front and walked in. Garza and Fogel were already there seated at the bar, facing the door. They showed no sign of recognition.

The bar itself was a large semi-circle. Crowded around it were rowdy hard drinking men and raucous women wearing short shorts, tank tops and cowboy hats. The women came there because the men always paid for their drinks, and they always got laid.

He scanned the room and saw the trap door that led to the attic crawl space. It was nailed shut and painted over many times. The tin ceiling above the bar was riddled with jagged bullet holes. Several layers of tin could be detected. New tin had been placed over the old ceiling a few times. There were tables off to the side where the weekend warriors sat. They were yuppies and suburbanites, who had heard about the bar and had come to slum. There weren't as many bullet holes in the ceiling there.

He scanned the bar for the guy called Lou. He saw what he was sure was his back at the video game console. He was tall, blonde, still and focused.

"Showtime," he told himself.

Approaching the video console Mickey morphed into the persona of a loud-mouthed clumsy jerk. He put his arm on Lou's shoulder and Lou recoiled.

"Hey man! Can two play this game?"

"No!" Lou replied knocking his arm from his shoulder.

Even though he had only spoken one word Mickey could hear that he had a hypnotic voice.

"Awww , come on. Play me! What's wrong? Are you afraid I'll out-maneuver you?"

"I prefer to play alone," Lou said dismissively, not taking his gaze from the screen. His hands masterfully clutched the steering wheel as he played "Death Race".

"That looks like fun. WOW! Yeah man! Grind them into the pavement. Watch them splatter! So cool! Hey! I've seen you before! I've seen you around. Wait a minute! I know you. Isn't your name Lou?"

A glint of paranoia came over Lou's otherwise unflinching gaze as he continued to play the game.

"No," he said.

"Sure it is! I know how I know you! I heard you singing Karaoke. The guy said, "Here's Lou singing, *I Will Follow You*. That was you. Right? Wow man, you're great! You could be a professional singer, Lou!'"

In an attempt to shut him up Lou said, "Luce. I prefer to be called Luce, not Lou."

"I never heard that name before. Are you from Europe or something?"

"It means 'light'."

"My name's Mickey, Luce."

"You neighborhood guys love the diminutive form...'Mickey'."

"What's that supposed to mean?"

"It means get lost Mickey. You're not my type."

"Wow man. I just came over here to have some fun. Who do you think you are? You can go to hell."

Luce looked up from the screen. This oaf couldn't have possibly guessed his little joke. His real name was Charles. He chose the name "Luce" for his game with Marissa.

"See ya, don't want to be ya," Mickey said to cement Luce's underestimation of him.

He walked over to the crowded bar where, thankfully, the bartender was too busy to notice him. He hated to waste money on a drink that he had no intention of drinking. He kept his eyes on "Luce". A few minutes had passed when everyone started looking at the clock. The second hand was moving toward midnight. A countdown began. Ten, nine, eight, seven, six, five, four, three, two, one...at the stroke of midnight someone shot his gun into the tin ceiling. The others immediately joined in the fun. Deafening gunfire filled the room. It all happened quickly. Luce never turned from the console. His grip tightened on the steering wheel as the drunken patrons whooped, hollered and shot in the air.

At the same time a weekend warrior hoisted a thick glass goblet of beer up high to make a drunken toast. Mickey's eyes went upward as a drop of blood fell from a bullet hole in the ceiling into the goblet turning the golden beer red.

"She's in the attic!" flashed in his mind like a lightning bolt. "This is a living video game!"

He looked at Luce. He had turned around and was looking at the goblet of red beer with an amused expression.

Mickey raced through the chaotic crowd to Garza and Fogel.

"Grab that guy and hold him for me," he screamed over the noise. They responded immediately.

Luce saw this exchange and bolted for the door with Fogel and Garza in hot pursuit close behind him.

The weekend warrior looked up to see that his beer was dark red. His gaze continued upward. He saw the blood dripping from the ceiling. Screaming in horror he threw the goblet across the room to the floor where it smashed, drenching the feet of the revelers at the bar in the bloody beer. The room went silent.

"Get into that attic," Mickey commanded the bartender. "There's someone up there. Somebody please call an ambulance!"

"It's been shut for decades," the frightened bartender blurted out. "It could take a while."

"Not with all of us helping," a muscled biker in a sleeveless vest called out.

Remembering the tree on the side of the building Mickey asked, "Are there any windows up there?"

"Yeah, but they've been boarded up for years."

"Tear open that trap door. I'm going to try to get in from outside. Someone, bring me a ladder."

Mickey raced outside to the back of the bar. Not waiting for the ladder he attempted to climb up the tree trunk. There were knots that could be used as footholds. As he climbed higher he found that there were hollowed out openings. The whole tree was teeming with rats. It was a rat's nest. He spotted a window that appeared to be boarded up. Holding onto a branch he reached out and pulled on a board. It swung to one side easily. The other boards did the same. The nails had been loosened. He raised the window with ease. Someone had been coming and going from here for quite some time. In the moonlight he could see a hammock and a pulley system hanging on the interior side of the window. As he climbed in, he was overcome by the stench of dead rodents. It was dark except for little beams of light that had been created by the bullet holes of the shooters. He could not stand up. He had to crawl. He could see the outlines of rats everywhere as they ran back and forth, squealing in a frenzy. As he slowly crawled, they ran over him with such speed that they felt like bursts of air. As he continued to crawl, he realized that some of the wooden planks had been gnawed away leaving the fiberglass insulation exposed. It felt stiff and sticky. He realized that it had been soaked with blood—blood that had dried.

Then he saw her. She was lying off to the side surrounded by rats. She had rolled there when the shooting started. She had followed the rats. She was very still. He prayed that she wasn't dead. As he crawled closer, he saw that she was bound and gagged. As he lifted her, a beam of light shown through the bullet hole she had passed out upon. He could feel her blood on his hands. She had been hit. He put his ear to her chest. He could hear her heart beating. He looked down to where she had been lying. The rats had eaten away all of the fiberglass from the small patch she had landed on, revealing the wood from the downstairs ceiling. There was no fiberglass in this spot to absorb the blood. That's why it trickled down through the bullet hole. If not for the rats, Marissa might not have been discovered. He thought about the dried blood he had felt. He wondered how much of it was from the dead rats and how much from other victims Luce had brought up there for this live version of his video game.

He could hear the pounding of the men downstairs prying open the trap door. He could hear the wail of the ambulance approaching and the sirens of police cars. As he took Marissa in his arms, the trap door fell open and bright light filled the attic. Squealing rats rained down on the men below, then scampered across the floor. He made his way to the trap door with Marissa in his arms and carefully lowered her down into the arms of the men who had batted away the deluge of rats, and waited with outstretched arms to assist in saving her life.

Fogel and Garza had captured Luce. He had been tripped by an overgrown tangle of roots that had defied their urban captivity under the sidewalk, cracking through it and lifting it a good foot off the ground.

Once Luce was down on the ground, a neighborhood dog began to viciously bark, alerting the officers to his exact location. Someone had called the police and squad cars were sitting outside with their lights flashing. Inside one sat Luce, bloodied, handcuffed and unblinking.

"Read him his rights," Mickey instructed the officers.

As the paramedics carried Marissa out on a stretcher Mickey added, "Get crime lab to work the bar. There may be more bodies up there."

The ambulance sped away taking Marissa to a nearby hospital. Mickey drove himself back to the detective unit. He was starving. His hands were covered in dried blood and rat piss, so he used a crumpled paper he found on the back seat to pick up his sandwich. He carried it into the building and put it in the break-room refrigerator. He was heading to his locker when he was stopped by one of the arresting officers,

"Here's the wacko's shit," the officer said as he handed him a manila envelope containing Luce's personal belongings. "For your report, we're beat 2513. Beat 2514 has the scene."

"Thanks", Mickey replied. "Did he give you any trouble?"

"Naw. We got him on a hook in the interrogation room," the officer said as he turned to leave.

Mickey made his way to his locker where he deposited the envelope, took out some clean clothes and went to wash up. When he had finished, he hungrily went to retrieve his sandwich, but someone had already eaten it.

"Goddam bastards," he thought.

He was ready to interview the prisoner. The sergeant briefed him as they stood outside the interrogation room.

"The girl is at Mercy Hospital. She is stable, but sedated and unresponsive. No need to follow up tonight. The nut job's name is Charles Aumeier. He lives in a pricey, luxury high rise on Lake Shore Drive. Garza and Fogel are over there now searching his place. So far we know that Charlie is a software developer for video games. He gets paid *beaucoup* bucks to make the kind of games you don't want your kids to play."

Mickey's mind flashed to the Bible: "...whose minds the gods of this age has blinded..."

"There weren't more bodies in the attic, but there was a lot of dried blood in the fiberglass. Some of it is from the rats that have been shot over the years. But we are sure there were other victims wounded up there. Crime lab is still working the bar. Charlie doesn't have a record but he was questioned a few days ago for—get this—the disappearance of a woman who used to be his agent."

"His agent," Mickey questioned. "You mean this guy's an actor too?"

"Or a model. We don't have that information yet."

"Is he married? Does he have a girlfriend, or a boyfriend?"

"No. He lives alone. Not even a pet. We're waiting to hear back from his condo board.

"Ok. I'm going in."

Mickey entered the small interrogation room where Luce sat calmly on a bench, handcuffed to a metal hoop on the wall. As Mickey un-cuffed him he said, "So we meet again, Luce," then with a grin he added, "I mean Charlie." He motioned to the table in the center of the room where they sat down across from each other. "Are there any other names you have that I should know about?"

"What do you think?"

"Umm...well...The Prince of Darkness. The Prince of the Power of the Air...Azazel?"

Charles just stared at him.

"The King of Tyre...Beelzebub...Satan?"

"Apollo," Charles replied

"Oh yeah," Mickey replied. "Apollo is in the stable of Satan isn't he? Okay Apollo. Tell me what happened. Feel free to quote the Bible. I spent most of my youth in catechism class so I speak the language."

"I like your dark humor," Charles replied in his mellifluous tone. "You're quite different from the jackass you pretended to be in the bar. Now that I've had a good look, I do know you. I have seen you falling in the void. You had lost your way. I have seen you on the battlefield. If only I had known. We could have been friends."

Mickey continued his interrogation.

"Let's cut the crap. We have Marissa. She's safe. Are there others?"

"Wouldn't you like to know."

"Why Marissa?"

"Oh come on copper. Isn't it obvious? We were both born of the Eterne. She is Venus to my Apollo. She dreams while she's awake like I do. She longs to be not solid flesh but 'transparent', written in light, like I am. He smiled as if responding to a private joke. "And we sing so pretty together. She belongs to me."

"And so you wanted to hurt her, because she belongs to you?"

"I wanted to elevate her. I wanted to introduce her to a whole new frequency. I wanted to purify her. Don't you know how purifying terror is, copper? Watch the young people playing my games. The more violence they inflict, the more ecstatic they become. The more adrenaline their deeds stimulate, the more clarity they experience. But Marissa wasn't like that, was she? She was so special. She was so angelic. Only I could awaken her most primitive instincts. Only I could add the missing notes to her angelic chord. I knew that she would love the experience of sheer terror...of exquisite pain. Did you feel her exquisite pain tonight, copper? It was a silent scream so intense that it became transcendent. It was a song. Did you hear it? Did it make your heart ache? It made my heart ache. It was intoxicating."

"Why the decapitated birds?" Mickey continued.

"They were my sacrifices to the 'Song Bird', perched up high in her magnificent nest, built so artfully of all that she had scavenged. The mirrors were a nice touch. Did you know that birds recognize their reflection in the mirror? They say it's proof of empathy."

"Why did you smash the crystal bird?" Mickey continued.

"To symbolize the closing of one chapter and the beginning of a new one. And, in the interest of total 'transparency', copper, I wanted to see what she looked like when she was terrified. She was breathtaking."

Mickey wasn't rattled. He had interrogated psychos before. "Did you rape her?"

Although remaining perfectly still Charles's mouth opened into a cavern as he laughed uproariously.

"Rape her? No I didn't rape her. Do I look like a man who has to rape women? I had my fill of carnal knowledge by the time I was twenty. Everyone wanted me. Women, men, young, old, rich...they begged me, they stalked me. They gave me whatever I wanted. Sex! I don't want sex anymore. It only brings me down."

"Yeah, you are a handsome guy. A man who looks like you could be a movie star."

"I have modeled. I was convinced to try it by a pathetic little creature who worshiped the ground I walked on. It was easy money. The narcissism and exhibitionism were a hoot at first. Then the others came. All of them thinking they were so slick and smart, none of them knowing how craven and obvious they really were. I turned them down. They had nothing to offer me. I have more money than I could ever spend. So why would I dress up in costumes and pretend to be someone else. That would be ludicrous when all anybody wants is to be me."

He looked right through Mickey and smiled a beautiful toxic smile.

"Did you take your agent to the Cowboy Bar?" Mickey asked.

"Oh copper. I took them all to the Cowboy Bar. It's so much fun there."

"How many?"

"That's for you to find out. That's your game. But I'll give you a hint. None of them die there."

"Why is that, Charlie?"

"I knew they wouldn't die there. There are several layers of tin covering a thick plank ceiling, a foot of fiberglass and a plank floor. Their wounds are never fatal. And they have the rats to show them what to do."

"I see. So you just do it for the fun."

"It's for them. I want them to feel fully alive for once in their lives. Afterwards it's really very touching to watch them experience their time of the end. The gradual realization that it was all a game. Their connection to me as the final witness to their life, and then, the submission to being rocked to sleep."

Mickey looked at him with contempt. "The Lord Rebuke Thee," he said.

"Oh Archangel," Luce replied with a smirk. "You just had to get your four words in! You sure know how to end a conversation." He leaned forward and his tone became conspiratorial. "I've given you your clues. The rest is for you to unravel. That's your fun."

"This isn't fun for me, Charlie. And you are not Lucifer. Lucifer was a teacher before he became a fallen angel. You are just a sick sadistic murderer."

"Oh come on Mickey. Let's do 'cut the crap'. You know where we are as well as I do. This is hell. You play your games and I'll play mine."

"This isn't hell, Charlie. Most people are good and aspire to be better. They are hard working, they love their families and are trying to do their best. But since you prefer hell, we're going to lock you away there for the rest of your life. You'll feel right at home. Everyone will want you."

Mickey stood up to leave.

"Have it your way 'Archangel Michael with the flaming sword'," Charlie said mockingly. "We both know the truth. The beast is hungry, and...'there is wickedness in heavenly places.'"

"That's Ephesians 6:12," Mickey said. Then he added:

" 'You are of your father, the devil, and the desires of your father you want to do. He was a murderer from the beginning, and does not stand in truth, because there is no truth in him. When he speaks a lie, he speaks from his own resources, for he is a liar and the father of it.' "

"That's from John 8:44."

Mickey liked to have the last word. He left the room.

He went home, showered, collapsed on his bed, and fell asleep hungry.

The next morning, Mickey was required to go to the hospital to see Marissa. He would have gone anyway. He wanted to see her. She was still sedated and unconscious. Her parents, Max and Elizabeth were with her. He introduced himself. They were very happy to meet him. He found them to be intelligent, kind and charming. They spoke with clarity and an economy of communication that Mickey appreciated. In his line of work he had listened to many people drone on without expressing a single coherent thought. Elizabeth played violin in the Chicago Symphony Orchestra and Max was an investment consultant who moonlighted playing jazz piano around the city. They expressed their gratitude at what he had done. They had hired a psychiatrist to talk with Marissa when she no longer needed to be sedated. She was in good hands. They would take good care of her. Mickey extended his hand to say goodbye. Elizabeth took him in her arms for a warm hug filled with gratitude. Max did the same.

"I feel like I know you," Max said. "The minute I saw you I thought I recognized you."

Mickey felt the same way but didn't tell him. He had to live in the real world. He left for another day of police work.

When he arrived at the detective's unit, Paul was waiting for him. He was anxious for an update on Marissa. They sat down together at one of the five communal desks and Mickey filled him in on what he could legally tell him.

"If I can help in any way, don't hesitate to call," Paul said. "If you need any keys identified or made, one of my side hustles is working as a locksmith."

"You're a locksmith?" Mickey repeated.

"Yeah", Paul said. "I repair clocks too."

"Just a second," Mickey told him.

Minutes later Mickey returned with the manila envelope. He poured its contents onto the desk: A wallet, some jewelry, a pen, a book of matches and Charlie's keys.

"Can you take a look at these keys for us?"

"No problem," Paul replied.

Paul looked through the keys identifying each one as the usual car, office and house key. Then he came upon a large one.

"This is the key to a boat," he told Mickey.

In a flash Mickey saw it all. The victims were "rocked to sleep" on a boat. He took the keys from Paul.

"Thanks," Mickey said as he hurriedly rose from his chair. "You've been a big help. I'll let you know what happens."

Mickey immediately began to research the boat key. He discovered that Charlie had a slip at Belmont Harbor where he kept his boat: "Death Racer"!

With sirens wailing Mickey and a team of officers and detectives descended on the Harbor. They quickly found "Death Racer" and inside its cabin a young woman bound and gagged, semi-conscious, covered in blood and starved. They identified her as Charlie's ex-agent, the woman who had been reported missing. Her name was Alicia. An ambulance was standing by. She was taken to nearby St. Joseph's hospital.

The next morning Mickey headed over to Mercy Hospital to check on Marissa. He couldn't get her out of his head. She raced through his thoughts like a speeding train, making his heart pound, and his body burn. He had entered into the minds of others while working on a case before, but they had never affected him like this. He had never gotten involved with those he met on the job, but this was different. He had been with many women, but he had never felt anything like this before. It was as if she was looking out of his eyes. It was something he couldn't identify or understand. Whatever it was, it had a life of its own. He couldn't control it. He ached to possess her.

He stopped in the gift shop and carefully picked out some flowers for her. When he entered her room, to his surprise, she was alone and although still attached to her intravenous feed, she was sitting up. She looked directly at him. The power of her gaze made him take a step backwards.

"Hello," she said. There was something familiar about him. "Do I know you?" she asked.

As he walked forward he felt the air moving as he passed through it. He had never met a woman with her own atmosphere before.

"I was assigned to your case," he said stopping at the foot of her bed.

"You're the man who found me," she said.

"Yes," he said.

"Yes," she said.

"These are for you," he said as he moved to the side of her bed. He extended the flowers to her.

She reached for them. Mickey did not let go. With both of their hands on the flowers they looked down at them and in an instant their perceptions shifted. They felt like they had taken some kind of mind-expanding drug. They saw the bouquet in startling detail. The flowers were in varying stages of blooming. Some still buds, tightly wrapped and struggling to push their way open into the light, others in fragrant full bloom, some starting to lose petals and go to seed, but alluring in their languid drooping. The colors and textures of the soft buds and velvety petals were so sensual that they wanted to caress them. They wanted to put their lips against them. Some were full of tenderness, some full of pulsing energy. All were bathing them with healing love. They looked up and as their eyes met, this madness extended into their bodies. They were plugged into the sun and melting into each other. Their excited bodies ached to be joined. They wanted to be naked in each other's arms. They yearned to put their hands on each other and touch every seen and unseen part. Their mouths ached to kiss and taste each other. Her eyes widened, his narrowed. They couldn't speak. It wasn't necessary. How long they were like this they couldn't tell. There was no time where they were. No past, no future, only now.

A doctor and his entourage broke the spell.

"How are you feeling today?" he asked as he briskly entered the room.

"Better," was all Marissa could say. It was clear that the doctor was there to examine her, and Mickey had to go to work. "I'll get out of your way, Doc," Mickey said, finding it hard to break eye contact with Marissa.

"Come back," was all she could say.

"I'll be back tomorrow," Mickey said, forcing himself to release the flowers and walk out the door.

Back at work he was briefed on the developments of the case. Alicia had been interrogated briefly before being sedated and was able to tell them that when she had been taken to the boat, there was a young man there, also bound and gagged. He lived for another day and then Charlie took the boat far out into Lake Michigan and threw him overboard. She had thought that she would be next. The police had sent out their divers to drag the lake. The body of a young man had been recovered.

He called Paul as he promised and gave him an update. Paul wanted to visit both women.

"You can try," Mickey told him. Marissa was awake this morning, but Alicia is sedated in the ICU. I don't know who they are letting in to visit at this point but tell them who you are. I'll call ahead and let them know how you helped us break the case."

When Paul arrived at Mercy Hospital Marissa had been taken to another floor for tests, so he headed back to the North Side to see if he would be allowed to see Alicia.

She was still unconscious and hooked up to several machines. Although her bullet wounds were soft tissue injuries, she had lost a lot of blood and had infections ravishing her body. In addition to this she was weak from starvation and dehydration. When Paul saw her he burst into tears. He had been told that her name was Alicia, but when he saw her he called out the name Alice. He began to sob uncontrollably. A nurse came to his aid and guided him to a waiting room with a couch.

"Is her name Alice?" he tearfully asked the nurse.

"No", she replied. "Her name is Alicia. Don't you know her?" The nurse could see that he was confused.

"I helped to find her," was all Paul could say.

"She's doing great," the nurse assured him. "She's getting all the care she needs to pull through."

"I don't know what's wrong with me," Paul began. "I suddenly thought her name was Alice," he sobbed. "Why do my fingers hurt?"

"You're in shock," the nurse told him. "Sit here and I'll get you some orange juice. That will help."

As the nurse hurried away Paul continued to sob. He didn't know why this affected him so deeply. He only knew that he wanted Alicia to recover with his whole heart and soul. It was crazy. He hadn't even met her, but still, she meant so much to him. He wanted to protect her. He wanted to take her in his arms. He felt so much love for her. He felt better after he drank the orange juice and was able to calm down. He went home, but never stopped thinking about Alicia.

The next day, Mickey went back to visit Marissa. He stopped and bought her another bouquet in the gift shop. When he entered her room a young man with sparkling brown eyes, dark hair half way down his back, a mustache, and a beard was with her. He was wearing a fringed jacket, a "Mr. Natural" t-shirt, fringed boots and lots of beads around his neck. He looked familiar. Mickey was sure he knew him. For a second he wanted to greet him with a bear hug. For a second tears welled up in his eyes.

"This is my brother Bob," Marissa said. "Bob this is Mickey, the detective who found me."

"Mickey," Bob greeted him taking his hand warmly. "I can't thank you enough."

He looked deep into Mickey's eyes and continued. "We share a great joy...and a great sorrow! This is a debt I can never repay. Maybe in the next life man. Maybe in the next life."

Mickey could see that Bob was high on some kind of drug.

"Bob is the lead singer for the rock band, 'Flight,'" Marissa said as if to explain. "He flew in from France when he found out about what happened to me."

"Yeah man," Bob said. "I have to fly back tonight. We've got gigs all over Europe. But I had to make sure my little sister was being taken good care of. You saved her life man. You saved her life."

"She saved her own life," Mickey told him. "She's a smart woman. She left clues. She knew to roll out of the way of gunfire. I just followed her clues."

It suddenly dawned on Mickey who Bob was. He was Bob Keyes, the Rock and Roll star whose song and album *The Lady Of The Lake* had gone Platinum! He was a Chicago boy who hit the big time. For years he had been in all the magazines and on all the late-night talk shows. He was a child prodigy who had been on his way to becoming a concert pianist when one day a fellow musician handed him an electric guitar... and a joint.

He had said in an interview, "Rock and Roll is my natural habitat. I like living at the intersection of chaos and clarity."

His comment wasn't pretension. He brought to the Rock genre

an emergent sound that was pure genius. His music intertwined nihilism and transcendence with so much energy that it could raise the dead. Yet there was also a haunting beauty that remained with the listener. It lingered like calming perfume in the air. It was a vision of salvation that accompanied the purge of nihilism. Mickey and his comrades used to listen to him while in Vietnam. And he was a favorite among the officers of the Chicago PD.

"I knew you looked familiar!" Mickey said. "I'm a fan from way back. I remember you guys playing at The Cellar in the sixties, before I went to Nam."

"Oh wow man! You were there!" Bob laughed with genuine camaraderie. "Those were the days! We were around fifteen years old when we were playing The Cellar!"

"Then you wrote *The Lady Of The Lake*, Mickey continued. "Great song man!"

"We really took off after that!" Bob commented. "We've been on the road ever since, traveling non-stop all over the world."

"It sounds exhausting," Mickey replied.

"We have our "Bolivian Marching Powder" to get us where we need to be," Bob joked. As they continued to talk, like long lost friends, Mickey noticed that Marissa remained silent. It was obvious that she and Bob were very close, but she did not support his lifestyle. She was worried about him. Mickey could feel her anguish.

Bob was a famous rock star and drugs were a component of the rock and roll lifestyle. He lived on the edge. He was an icon of the "Counter Culture". People flocked to him. They wanted him to transport them to the crazy atmospheres that he inhabited and documented in his compositions. They wanted to party with him. They envied him. He was showered with adulation and approval for being stoned all the time. And he was intrigued by the drug-induced realms that he visited. It made her angry. It made her feel helpless. Bob was walking a tight rope, high up over a dangerous landscape. He was being cheered on by millions of people who wanted to watch him defy death for their own excitement. People who would forget about him and quickly move on if he fell to his death. Mickey understood Marissa's anxiety. He was saddened by Bob's addiction too. He sensed that Marissa wanted time alone with her brother.

"I'll let you have some time with your brother," Mickey said. "I know he has to leave soon, so I'll be on my way." He put the flowers on the table by Marissa's bed. They exchanged an intimate look full of longing.

Bob threw his arms around Mickey in a long embrace. "I love you man," he said.

To his surprise Mickey said, "I love you too man."

Mickey was deeply moved by meeting Bob. He had known Bob as a public figure, but there was something else about him that he was struggling to remember. He felt sure he had known him before, somewhere else. It haunted him throughout the day but the memory was just out of reach. He couldn't grasp it.

He also thought about how insidious and destructive the drugs that Bob was taking were. He wanted to stage an intervention. He had just met him, but the thought of losing him to an overdose was more than he could bear. He wanted Bob to live a long and happy life. He didn't want him to die young. Maybe he would talk to Marissa about it at some point. He hoped Bob would be all right.

The next morning he was back at the hospital with another bouquet of flowers.

This time Marissa was alone. They began to talk with each other. They had nothing in common but it didn't matter. Just the sound of each other's voices and the look in each other's eyes was the real conversation. They laughed together over little things. Nothing was trivial. Everything was insanely interesting and funny and perfect, and painfully tender. Mickey put flowers in Marissa's hair and kidded her about Haight-Ashbury.

He sang:
"If you're going to San Francisco
Be sure to wear some flowers in your hair..."

"You have a beautiful voice," she told him.

"Me?" he laughed. "I was an altar boy. I sang the Mass in Latin. I fool around on the drums a little for my own amusement. That's about it for my musical career."

Then he arranged the rest of the flowers on the bed, surrounding her, while she looked on entranced. She thought he was hilarious, kind, brave, and utterly charming. She felt completely natural with him. He came back every day for the next week.

Other bouquets started to arrive from friends and relatives. Soon her room was filled with flowers. Seeing her in a room filled with flowers stirred a distant memory in Mickey. It was like an echo that was too far away to understand, but could be heard.

He could only touch her gently for she was still bandaged and in pain. He touched her hands and her face with his fingertips sending both of them soaring with warm sensations. Then after a few more days he softly kissed her lips. This soft kiss ignited a forest fire in their bodies. They were burning up with desire. They were waiting for the day when they could make love.

2

Marissa finally came to her exit off the expressway. She heaved a sigh of relief. Now she only had to navigate the deserted local streets, left pitch black by a power failure. This was child's play compared to what she had just been through. She couldn't wait to get home to Mickey. It wasn't far to his home now. She would be safe in his arms soon. He would hold her close. The spell of the highway was broken. The phrase "a binding veil of rain" was now an artifact. She made a mental note to tell her brother Bob to write a song with that title. It suited his musical style. What she had heard, spoken in the rain, was respectfully relegated to a back burner in her mind, as the joy of the very real, vivid memories of the not to distant past flooded through her. Her body was now awake, electrified by the memory of the first time she and Mickey made love.

Two weeks passed before she was discharged from the hospital. Her parents wanted her to come to their home in the suburbs, but upon Marissa's insistence they drove her to her own apartment. She was anxious to be with her cat Morgan le Fay, and she and Mickey had made a date for a few days later. He was taking her to Chez Paul for a celebratory dinner.

On the evening of their date Mickey left his neighborhood early. Parking was always difficult in Rogers Park and he didn't want to be late. He wanted everything to be perfect. As he walked up the three flights of stairs to her apartment, with a beautiful bouquet of flowers, to his surprise, his heart was pounding. He knocked on her door...and there she was! He had never seen her standing up before! She was wearing a form fitting sapphire blue dress with a "V" neckline. She looked like a goddess. At her feet was a purring Morgan le Fay. The intensity of her gaze almost knocked him back down the stairs. She took his breath away.

"Come in," was all she could say.

He stepped inside and she closed the door. They both stood there, their eyes locked together, riveted, burning with desire.

"These are for you," was all he could say as he extended the flowers to her.

As she reached for the bouquet, a dam burst inside both of them and all reason was lost. In this electrical storm of urgent, immediate need, the bouquet was thrown to the floor and their mouths met in deep hungry kisses.

As they kissed all things hidden inside her emerged and spun around her like a chrysalis. All doubt, fear, cruelty, shame, malice, loneliness, pain, outcast status, and poverty in all its forms spun about her with such velocity that they shattered into meaningless shards. She emerged as a butterfly, flying free, lit by phosphorescent colors. This was ecstasy. Making love with him brought her to the center of her being, where no compromised or chaotic element could exist. This was the high country that lovers seek. The place of divine madness where the angels, and the sentient beings fueled by pure love live. They were beyond the inventions of culture, and all that substituted appearing to be, for becoming. They were joined to the higher realms.

They made love four times that night. At first delirious and frenzied, then intense and tender, then joyful and full of laughter, then sweet, soft and loving. From that night on they were inseparable. Their bodies and souls were tuned to one another for a lifetime. Afterwards, as they rested in each other's arms in the dark, they were surrounded by the whispers of centuries, lulling them into a peaceful twilight sleep. They both thought, "I am the luckiest person on earth".

The memory filled her with aching bliss. She was growing impatient. She was close to Mickey's house now. The rain was still coming down hard. It was hard to remember where the side streets were in the dark, but slowly she was finding her way.

3

Mickey had just finished his bitter lemon when the lights went out. The velocity of the wind had felled a tree, which knocked out a power line, plunging the neighborhood into darkness. He went out into the storm to line his driveway with big, yellow, industrial flashlights, hoping that they would serve as a beacon to help Marissa find his house. He went back inside and waited for her. The lightning lit up the wall of his living room where a painting he had purchased in Paris hung. It was a picture of the French countryside. He had found it in an antique shop while on military leave in France. It was out of character for him to buy a painting. Especially one so expensive and that he would have to ship back to the States. He never understood why he was so drawn to this painting, but it quickly became one of his prized possessions. He had spent many nights gazing at the painting, contemplating the sensitive hand that had rendered it. His eyes went to the artist's signature in the right hand corner: Daniel Petelle. Now, for just a second, he thought how familiar that name seemed, and how beautiful this artist's creation looked lit by the lightning. A loud explosion of thunder made his mind jump to another memory. It was far away on a battlefield. It was frightening, but gone before he could grasp it.

His mind returned to Marissa. Worried, he paced up and down in front of the window, watching for her headlights in the dark. Finally he saw her car pulling into his driveway. He went out to greet her with an umbrella, sheltering her from the rain, grateful that she was home, safe and sound.

Marissa would tell him of her journey in the storm, and of the word spoken to her by the rain. But not now. Now the need to quiet the urgent aching of her body in Mickey's embrace was all that mattered. The hidden currents that had been ignited in both of them by the storm combined into one force, seeking expression in touch and sensation, eager to impart all the information they held wordlessly, in the act of the union of their bodies. Mickey took her in his arms and held her close. In the soft glow of the many candles he had lit, he wanted to say beautiful words to her. But he was a detective, not a poet. He sat her down in his velvet armchair under the antique painting of the French countryside. He knelt at her feet and opened a small box containing a diamond ring. He wanted to tell her how much he loved and cherished her. But all he could say was, "Marry me".

Marissa slid off the velvet chair into his embrace.

"Yes, I'll marry you," she whispered reverently, knowing that to be his wife was her heart's deepest desire.

As he slid the ring onto her finger, the lifetimes of abstinence and prayer, of mystical participation and ascendance, fame, romance and propriety, achievement, profound companionship, love, loss and devastating pain surged through them both. Tonight their passion for one another would know no bounds. They clung to each other as the wind howled around them, rattling the windows, and the rain pounded down on the roof while the thunder boomed, followed by brilliant flashes of lightning that made the living room strobe, interrupting the soft candle glow. On the floor they made love with a fury equal to the wild ravages of the storm, as it felled neighborhood trees and blew off roofs. They danced this wild dance, primordial and holy, all night, until both they and the storm were depleted. They were finally at peace. They were home. They had come to this present moment of total fulfillment by way of hundreds of years and the lifetimes that still lived within them. They were fully present in eternity. They were fully flesh and spirit. They were fully human.

As they lay in each other's arms, sleeping on the floor, Mickey had a dream. He was back in Marissa's apartment the night of the abduction. He was kneeling on the floor examining the shattered crystal bird. Suddenly all the pieces of the crystal bird came flying back together until he was holding it in his hand. Then before his eyes it turned into a living bird: a beautiful, large white bird. It perched on his hand for a second then spread its wings, and flew straight up into the air, for there was no longer a ceiling. It flew into the night sky, lit by thousands of stars and circled above him. Then Marissa was there, kneeling beside him and he was putting the diamond ring on her finger. As they knelt there the white bird descended and hovered over them, calling out, blessing them.

4

Chicago ~ 1970's, 1980's 1990's and beyond

Marriage bought to Mickey and Marissa a resting place for their souls. It was a place of perfect peace, but not of slumbering. It was not the end of their journey, but only the end of their wandering. Life held many more lessons for them.

They had been part of a generation who had unraveled the orthodoxies of the past, searching for meaning in the natural world, literature, poetry, music, politics, justice and ancient practices. They had sought liberation from cultural mores, rejecting that which they felt was shame-based and hypocritical. Now the times were rapidly changing, and society was once again reconfiguring itself. They had become parents. It was now their responsibility to provide stability within their family, while remaining the "change agents", that had been the identity of their generation.

They had a daughter whom they named Gretel. She was diagnosed at three years of age with a learning disability. Marissa and Mickey devoted themselves to researching her condition. After two years they discovered that she had food allergies, which mimicked the symptoms of psychological and physiological disorders. Her allergies could be overcome with a change of diet. By the time Gretel was ready for school her mind was as clear as a bell, and their gratitude was overflowing. As a family they were not spared the disappointments, injustices, heartbreaks and petty tyrannies of life. But with love as their animating force they were a very joyful and optimistic family.

Mickey continued his career with the Chicago Police Department, risking his life daily to save the lives of others while maintaining law and order. When he kissed Marissa goodbye every morning they both knew that they might be seeing each other for the last time. This kept them living in the present moment.

Marissa continued to do her hologram art but eventually couldn't find funding for new projects. She became a folk singer, often joined onstage by Mickey. She also sat in as vocalist for her father's jazz sets around the city. Marissa and Mickey attended church, but they didn't believe in the exclusivity of any one religion. They accepted that there are many paths to experiencing unity with the divine.

As the years progressed from the late 1970's into the next decade, Marissa observed that many people were beginning to turn away from worship. What was natural, sustaining and revitalizing to her, was considered to be unknowable and of no interest to more and more people. Many began to speak of belief in the Divine as a superstition, preferring to live a secular lifestyle.

It was during this time that the technology, which had been steadily growing since the development of the transistor in 1947, introduced the personal computer and the Internet, plunging the world into a tidal wave of information. Marissa and her family had to adapt. They learned to work on computers and then to carry cell phones. The phone booths of the past were being taken away, Marissa sometimes wondered if that phone booth in the middle of nowhere, that had been lit by lightning so many years ago, was still there. She longed to enter it one more time.

It was disturbing to her that people were spending so much time alone on their computers, and would now rather "text" than speak to one another. She saw it as an addiction that made people readily choose isolation rather than the shared experiences of the past.

Marissa witnessed futility, pessimism, and fanaticism dominating a world that was losing its grip on the spiritual universe. It was woven into the fabric of her being that mystical participation in life was the greatest gift given us during our time on earth. But now, instead of holding tight to our human connection to the divine, society was choosing to connect to multiple electronic screens, which taught them to replace seeming for being. As she watched this transition she feared that eventually connection to machines would become more desirable than human connection to one another, and that digital creations would create a principality of ideas to replace the fundamental narratives of divinity.

Marissa had made her home in the abstract regions of artistry. The origins of her work with holograms had been facilitated by technology. But what was happening in the world now was unexpected and threatening. She often discussed it with Mickey: "The foundation of science is an irrational faith that there is an intelligent structure to the universe. So isn't God the precondition that fuels science?" she would ask. "Doesn't every scientific quest eventually lead to a 'point of miracle'? Why is this fundamental truth being forgotten?"

Mickey, who in his work had witnessed the worst of what human beings were capable of, would reply, "The human race is fundamentally good. Collectively we will overcome the tyrannical impulses of those who would use technology for evil intent." His words, based on experiential wisdom, always gave her strength.

Still she asked herself if growing old was not about losing one's youth, but losing the world you once knew and loved, and having what you know to be essential and true, discarded.

These melancholy moods would pass. Through their discussions,

Mickey and Marissa were both growing in their comprehension of the complexities of this new age, and evolving in their ability to be knowledgeable participants in it. They had become excited about the potential uses of the incredible innovations of the computer age to solve problems that were beyond human calculation.

Now, through their discussions, they realized that their words had been giving form to what had been deep stirrings in their souls. Once again, something, just out of reach, was calling out to them. It became stronger. It preoccupied them. Sometimes it kept them up at night. It felt like a call to action, but they couldn't bring it into focus. They prayed for guidance.

In the early nineties it was reported in the news that prophets from a small town in Bosnia called Medjugorje, were having visions of the Blessed Virgin Mary.

People of all faiths, from all over the world, were flocking there to witness this miraculous event. It was documented that many were being healed as they gathered there to pray.

The prophets announced that they were instructed by the Blessed Virgin to come to Hillside Cemetery in Chicago, where she would appear to the faithful who gathered there. Marissa and Mickey felt sure that this was the guidance that they had been seeking.

When the day finally came they stood at the very back of the crowd, observing along with hundreds of the faithful, as the prophets stood reverently looking at what they described to be a vision of the Blessed Virgin accompanied by many angels.

After the worshipers recited prayers together, the prophets turned and looked out over the crowd. They looked directly at Marissa and Mickey, way in the back, and motioned for them to come forward. After an initial moment of surprise they obeyed, and as the crowd parted they made their way to the sacred space where the prophets stood before the Blessed Virgin. Once there, the prophets reverently anointed them with oil. As they stood, hand in hand, before the apparition, a feeling came over them of not being solid, but fluid and flowing in a powerful sea of healing grace. Their eyes closed and their faces were drawn upward by a light that was so alive that it resonated with warmth. What felt like a wind rushed through their bodies stirring every cell to cognizance Their lungs expanded, rising and falling like the movement of wings, connecting them to the flight of the angels, while grounding them to their bodies, and to the earth. Their only impulse was to reach out to share this ecstatic joy and profound sense of knowing with others. They knew beyond question that it was this force that animates the desire for human connection. They heard the murmur of the worshipers who had begun to pray. Through the sound of their words their hearts were joined and began to beat as one. They felt the ascension of their souls into one divine force, at one with each other and with all of creation. While in this transcendent state the prophets whispered that the Blessed Virgin had a message for them: "Pray for Peace on Earth."

The lessons of all their lifetimes had prepared them for this moment, and for all that was to come. For the rest of their lives they would pray that all would come to know this joy, and be alive in this spirit of reaching out, knowing that to share the resources of the earth in peace, without greed, prejudice or exclusivity of belief systems, is the evolution of the human journey from survival to enlightenment. They dedicated themselves to this quest. They were filled with a profound feeling of satisfaction. Their journey had come full circle.

5

Epilogue

A CONCERT OF SOULS

Marissa's neighbor Paul married Alicia and together they ran a successful talent agency and graphic arts business. He took her to Sardinia for their honeymoon where they conceived a child whom they named Claudio. He was a wild, fun-loving child, who with their love and attention grew into a kind-hearted adult. Under his father's tutelage he became a cartoonist, famous for his edgy, surreal renderings. They had another child named Anna. Claudio gave her the nickname "Anna-Zanna" or "Zanna" for short. She was a very loving child. She would dance around their home singing, "I love you, I love you, I love you". Although she was younger than Claudio she loved to take care of him, and it warmed his heart. She had a love for music and pursued it with such devotion that at a young age she became an accomplished musician proficient on several instruments. She became a nun, joining a teaching order, The Sisters of Saint Joseph, where she taught music and was beloved of thousands of children

Claudio married Marissa and Mickey's daughter, Gretel, who had grown up to become a popular writer of children's books. When Max and Elizabeth grew too old to live alone they moved in with Mickey and Marissa, and were cherished till their dying day. Both families remained the closest of friends, sharing all of life's moments, great and small, for the rest of their lives. Often they would remark, "How did we get so lucky? We must have some really good karma!"

From time to time they would talk about Charles and how he, a homicidal psychopath, had been the catalyst that brought them all together. A strange and chilling realization, but one that they didn't want to ignore. Charles remained in prison for the criminally insane, where under close scrutiny, he wrote computer programs for the prison system. At times the FBI would call upon him to assist in solving abduction cases. Then one morning the prison guard found him dead in his cell. He had hanged himself. He left a note that read, "Karma's a bitch."

Bob enjoyed his Rock and Roll fame for the rest of his life. Over the years there were several interventions, and several stays in rehab, before he continued his career drug free. His album, *A Blinding Veil Of Rain* topped the charts for many months and went Platinum. Along with *The Lady Of The Lake,* it was considered a classic. He married a concert pianist named Jennifer and they had a son whom they named Arthur. One Christmas his parents gave Arthur a bulldog named Pendragon, who became his constant companion. Arthur and Pendragon accompanied them on their concert tours, where Arthur learned every aspect of producing. Eventually he opened his own production company that he named "Excalibur."

Years earlier, when Bob returned to his European tour after Marissa's abduction, he had been hired to perform for a private party at the villa of an older couple from the Italian aristocracy. Enamored of him, they gave him one of their treasures. It was a very old book of sacred music. Seeing that it was hundreds of years old, Bob considered giving it to a museum. But when he received the news of his sister's engagement to Mickey he knew that this must be his wedding gift to them. It was because on the inside cover there was a faded drawing of a man who looked just like Mickey! The inscription was faded too, but still legible. It was inscribed:

"Love is eternal, and eternity is now".

Finis

GLOSSARY OF INCARNATIONS

PART ONE	PART TWO	PART THREE
Gretchen/Sister Mary Theresa	Theresa	Marissa
Father Michael	Salvatore DeCarlo/Father Michael	Mickey
Robert	Robert	Bob
The Duke of Mecklenburg	Claude	Claudio
Elizabeth	Elizabeth	Elizabeth
Choirmaster of the Cathedral	Maximillian	Max
Gretchen (died in childbirth)	Greta	Gretle
	Marzanna	Anna-Zanna
The former Duke of Mecklenburg	Charles	Luce/Charles
Father Theodore	Pastor Theodore	
	Paolo	Paul
	Alice	Alicia
Forest animal	Merlin	Morgan le Fay
Father Michael's horse	Gwydion	Pendragon
	Danielle Petelle	Creator of Michael's painting